Heartfully
Galatea Matter

M. Aishvarya

Invincible Publishers

First published in India in 2017 by Invincible Publishers

ISBN: 978-93-86148-39-1

Invincible Publishers
F-55, Sushant Lok II, Hong Kong Bazar Lane Sector 57,
Gurgaon-122003

Opposite Kasturba Ashram, Radaur Distt Yamuna Nagar, Haryana- 135133

DEDICATION

To my parents, who kept inspiring me .

Acknowledgment

* * *

I acknowledge my work to OVID , the classical Roman Poet , whose work inspired me to bring this book to shape and size.

Chapter 1
The crowd

* * *

2013

BHUBANESWAR RAILWAY STATION

There was a large crowd in front of the ticket counter. Haksh and his friend Chinmay were standing in the queue.

"I think we should've booked the ticket yesterday," said Haksh.

"Have patience. The queue will end," said Chinmay.

"By the time I reach the counter the train will leave."

"But why are you worrying? You have to go to Sambalpur, not Mumbai. If you miss the train today, you will get another tomorrow."

"That gives me an idea."

The boys waited for a long time in order to reach the counter. An announcement was made about some train leaving the railway platform.

"There goes the train I was waiting for,"said Haksh, heaving a sigh out of disappointment. He took out some money from his pocket and asked the man at the ticket counter about the next train to Sambalpur.

"Tapaswini Express," said the man at the counter.

"When will it come to Bhubaneswar?" asked Haksh

"Night."

"Book a ticket for me in any train that is going to

Sambalpur tomorrow."

Haksh got a ticket booked to Sambalpur.

"Madan told me to book the ticket early; only I was too lazy to do that," said Haksh while walking out of the railway station. "He told me about the crowd. The crowd may create a problem for me in catching the train"

"But why are you in a hurry to go to **Sambalpur** ?" asked Chinmay.

"The new academic session has started and I have to keep a decent attendance in order to be in the good books of the teachers," said Haksh.

"Forget about it and chill in my room. ," said Chinmay.

"Yes," said Haksh. "You're right."

The two boys got into an auto rickshaw and left the railway station area. Haksh was looking angrily at the crowd of people who were heading towards the railway station. He was upset over missing the train to Sambalpur because of the crowd. There was definitely something for which he wanted to reach Sambalpur early.

2013

INSIDE CHINMAY'S ROOM

Chinmay and Haksh entered a colony. They halted in front of a building, which was a dorm where Chinmay lived. After having their supper, Haksh lay on the floor while Chinmay climbed on **to** the bed.

"I feel bad that you are lying on the floor. Why don't you sleep on my bed like other days ? I will sleep on the floor as I have been doing all these days," said Chinmay.

" Not today .You sleep on the bed. It belongs to you. "

"Why not?"

" No definite reason."

Chinmay could feel there was some sort of disappointment in Haksh's voice.

"Haksh, why do you sound disappointed?" asked Chinmay.

"I've a friend named Madan who once told me about the legend of Pygmalion and Galatea. I am disappointed about that," said Haksh.

"Why does that legend disappoint you ?" asked Chinmay.

"Pygmalion was a sculpture .Once he made a statue of a beautiful lady. He fell in love with the statue and wished it were real. He searched everywhere but **could** not find any girl who was as beautiful as the statue. He cried. Aphrodite heard him and blessed the statue. The statue began to get life. It began to respond to Pygmalion's love." said Haksh.

"What is the reason for being sad about it?"

"The girl I love is no less than a statue. She is as emotionless as a statue. Madan has told me if I help love couples like you, then something may take place in my life. I wonder what will take place with me after I've helped people like you ."

"That's a strange logic."

"For a drowning man even a straw is a big thing. Madan's words have given me hope.I want that girl to acknowledge my love and respond to me. If not her lover, then I am ready to be her friend. "

The two boys talked about various legends that involved lovers before sleep overcame them.

FEBRUARY, 2006
A GARDEN IN PADAMPUR

The summer season is very hot. The heat of the sun has become very difficult to tolerate because of global warming. The summer season is something very funny in villages.

In villages, children enjoy the summer. They take a dip in the ponds and rivers at any time of the day in order to beat the heat. Some of these children would be busy playing games, but the **favourite** pastime for the village kids is throwing stones at the mangoes. Mangoes are consumed in large quantities during the Summer season. The **children** gather under the mango trees and try to bring down as many mangoes as possible by throwing stones at them.

Some school children, who were in their early teens, stood outside the boundary wall of a garden. Two children knelt on the ground. Two children stood on the shoulders of the other two children. The rest of the children supported the two children who were standing. The ones who were kneeling down stood up slowly. Now the boys who were standing on the shoulders of the two children could catch the top of the boundary wall. They hung from the wall. After much effort they crossed the wall. The other side of the wall had a lot of grass. The children , who scaled the wall ,fell on the grass.

"Mishra Babu is increasing the height of the wall every year. Last year it was easy to cross it ,"said Haksh, who was one of the two children who scaled the wall. He took out a rope from his school bag.

"Bring a stone," said Haksh to his companion.

The companion picked up a stone from the ground and gave it to Haksh. The latter tied one end of the rope to the stone and threw the stone across the wall. The stone flew across the wall, taking one end of the rope with it. One of the boys standing outside the wall held the rope tightly. Haksh and his companion held the rope tightly **from** inside the wall and began to pull the rope. Along with the rope they pulled one more boy into the boundary wall of the garden. Some more boys were pulled into the garden using the same process.

When the boys inside the boundary wall became ten, the rope was not used anymore. The ten boys walked about in the garden.

There was a mango orchard in the garden. The boys

entered it.

"You all go up. I am keeping a watch. If I see the watchman, I will raise an alarm." said Haksh.

The boys climbed the mango trees and began to pluck the mangoes. While keeping vigil Haksh heard a giggling sound.

"Who is giggling?" said Haksh to himself. He heard the faint giggling again. He walked some steps ahead and saw two girls standing under a mango tree. They were throwing stones at the mangoes.

One girl was in dappled frock and the other was in a pink frock. Haksh stood where he was and kept looking at the girl in pink frock. For some reason a smile broke on his face.

"Are you able to see the watchman anywhere?" asked one of his friends from the tree.

"If my friends keep shouting like this, I cannot remain here longer," said Haksh, thoughtfully.

He looked at his friends who were on the mango trees. He took out a red towel from his school bag and waved it. This was a signal. His friends climbed down the tree and ran towards the boundary wall.

When the boys had run away from the mango trees, Haksh put the towel in his bag and looked at the two girls. His attention was focussed on the girl in pink frock. The two girls were throwing stones at the mangoes. Till now they had collected a handful of mangoes. After sometime, they collected the mangoes that had fallen on the ground and walked away. Haksh ran towards the wall. He saw one of his companions sitting on the boundary wall.

"What were you doing inside the garden after we left ?" asked the boy.

"That's none of your business," said Haksh.

The boy lowered the rope and pulled Haksh up.

Once Haksh was out of the garden , the boys

dispersed after sharing the mangoes. Haksh looked at the garden and smiled before heading to his home.

Chapter 2
The exams

* * *

FEBRUARY,2006
PADAMPUR

Haksh reached home before sunset. He entered the kitchen and gave his mother two mangoes. She asked him from where he had got the mangoes.

"A friend gave me," said Haksh.

"Did you get it from a friend, or did you steal it from Mishra Babu's garden?" asked Nabin, Haksh's elder brother. He was standing behind Haksh. "I saw you and your friends. You people had gathered outside the boundary wall of Mishra Babu's garden."

Haksh knew he had been caught and there was no way to escape.

"Why do you have to steal things, Haksh?" said Mrs. Namita, the mother of Haksh and Nabin.

"Sorry, Maa," said Haksh with his head downcast.

"What is there in saying sorry to me. If someday Mishra babu catches you, you'll definitely get the beating of your life. So, change your habits." said Mrs. Namita.

"What happened?" said Mr Bijay, entering the kitchen. "Why are you all talking about Mishra Babu? Did Haksh steal mangoes from his garden?"

"Yes," said Mrs. Namita.

Mr Bijay was the father of Haksh and Nabin.

"Haksh, it is not good to steal. If you keep this habit then you will be hated in the society someday." said Mr Bijay to Haksh.

That night, after having supper Haksh was unable to sleep properly. Whenever he closed his eyes he saw the face of the girl in pink frock in Mishra Babu's garden and his sleep broke. Mr Bijay was a high school teacher in a government school, Mrs Namita was a housewife, Nabin was the elder son of the family and Haksh was the younger son. Nabin was a student of class ten and Haksh was a student of class seven. This was the family of Mr Bijay.

APRIL, 2006
PADAMPUR

The new academic session started. Haksh had to change his school as his previous school could only take students up till class seven. He followed his brother's footsteps and joined the Town High School.

It was the month of April. Nabin was to join a college for his higher secondary studies. Mr. Bijay was happy over Nabin going to college for his further studies. He wanted to gift his son for doing well in the board examinations of class ten. He purchased a of TVS Star bike for Nabin.

"I wish I could get a chance to ride it" said Haksh on seeing the bike.

MAY, 2006
PADAMPUR

It was May, the time of summer vacations. Haksh told his brother that he wanted to play in the big open field which was not far from the house. Till that time the boy used to play in the small playground that was near the house.

"Why are you telling that to me? It's your wish" said Nabin. "You can go to the big field to play. No one is objecting you."

Haksh and his friends went to the big playground in the colony. There, Haksh befriended a few, one of whom was Chinmay. He was a student of **Saraswati Sishu Vidyamandir**, a school located in the town of Padampur.

Chapter 3
The dam

* * *

JULY, 2006
PADAMPUR

The classes reopened and Haksh got busy with his lessons.He had covered a significant part of his syllabus during the summer vacation. This was going to help him a lot. He had his hands full with school and tuition taking most of his time. On a vacant day, he decided to get along with his friends..

Some boys with bicycles gathered near his house.

"You all stand here. I am going to call Haksh," said one of the boys and walked towards the front door of Haksh's house. He knocked the door. Mrs. Namita opened the door and looked at that boy.

"Namaste, Aunty!" said the boy. "I'm Digvijay, Haksh's friend."

Digvijay sat in the front room while Mrs. Namita called Haksh. Haksh entered the room and they both shared **pleasantries** and went outside to meet the whole team.

"Where are we going then?" asked Haksh.

"We are going to the dam in Barikel. Would you like to accompany us?" asked Digvijay.

"You know what, today I was thinking of visiting you guys. Thank God that you guys came. I will definitely come," said an overjoyed Haksh.

Haksh went inside, got ready and left for the dam. Barikel had a dam in it. The boys were going to see the dam. It was a local favourite for anyone going for sightseeing. Haksh sat on Chinmay's cycle carrier.

"Ride!" said Haksh.

"Okay," said Chinmay and began to pedal the cycle.

All the boys were riding their bicycles in a straight line,one following the other in order to avoid being hit by the vehicles plying on the road. Chinmay was the last cyclist in the line.

"I am the last in the line because of your sitting on my carrier," said Chinmay.

"Don't be so sad, mate. We are going on sightseeing. This is not a cycle race," said Haksh.

The boys had to pass in front of the Saraswati SishuVidya Mandir school. It was four or four- thirty p.m in the afternoon. The classes were over and the children were coming out of the school.

There was a big rush in front of the school. Chinmay was cycling slowly in the busy traffic and Haksh was enjoying the sight of children eating fast food.A girl was coming on a bicycle from the front . She was in white salwar and navy-blue kameez with a white dupatta covering her shoulders. Haksh's eyes fell on the girl. The girl had tied her hair in two bunches with two ribbons. She crossed Chinmay's bicycle. Haksh kept looking at her for a long time.

"I think I have seen her somewhere," said Haksh to himself.

He tried to recall. After some seconds he remembered the girl in pink frock whom he saw in Mishra Babu's garden.

"Oh, dear, it's that girl!" said an elated Haksh.

"Which girl?" asked Chinmay.

"Nothing." said Haksh.

"No, you mentioned the word 'girl', so tell me which girl?"

"Why? What's the matter?"

"No, nothing"

"Then why are you asking **?**"

"A girl from our school has got your attention. That's interesting"

"Just shut your mouth and keep pedalling. Our friends have gone ahead. We have to catch up with them. Pedal speedily"

"Okay, okay"

Chinmay did not ask anything further and kept pedalling. The boys reached the Barikel dam. They enjoyed the sight. They all had a conversation going on, but Haksh looked lost. He

remained silent, listening to his friends. At about five-fifteen or five-twenty p.m in the evening the boys left the dam and returned to their respective homes. Chinmay left Haksh in front of the latter's home. There was a bright smile on the face of Haksh. He ran into his house. After washing his legs he sat with his books. Before reading his books, he closed his eyes and began to think about the incident that took place in front of SSV School. He thought about the girl whom he had seen there and smiled. He opened his eyes and tried to read his course book, but, was unable to focus his mind. While reading his book he had a huge grin on for no apparent reason. At the dining table Nabin noticed Haksh smiling.

"What's the matter, Haksh? Why are you smiling?" asked Nabin.

"Nothing,Brother," said Haksh. He ate his share of food quickly and went to bed. He lay on the bed and covered his face with the blanket. He shut his eyes and began to think about the girl. He did not know why he felt happy whenever he thought about that girl. For some days, he kept changing sides to get good sleep, but no sleep came to his eyes.

Chapter 4
Bike riding

* * *

JULY, 2006
AN OPEN FIELD IN PADAMPUR

It was Sunday. The dew drops had made the grass wet. Haksh and Mr Bijay were in the field with the new bike. Haksh always saw Nabin ride the bike, so he began to wish he could ride the bike too.

One day he told his mother that he wanted to learn bike riding. Mrs Namita like any other mother talked to his father about it.

"Nabin is mature. I am not worried if he rides the bike. Haksh is completely different. The kind of nuisance he does leaves me worried" said Mr Bijay.

"You teach Haksh bike riding, but make sure that you put some rules and regulations on him" suggested Mrs Namita.

Mr Bijay accepted the suggestion. He decided to teach Haksh bike riding on Sundays. On the days when he was busy , it was Nabin who taught Haksh how to handle the bike. Time passed and Haksh learnt to ride the bike.

AUGUST, 2006
PADAMPUR

One day a thought occurred to Haksh. "What if

I ride the bike alone?" he thought. He began to daydream about how he would be riding his bike on the road and how his friends would be looking

at him. They would ask him for a ride.

One day when Haksh was returning from school he saw a bike borne young couple. The boy was holding the bike's handle and the girl had put her hands around the young man's waist. Both were chatting while riding the bike. After seeing this, Haksh began to imagine many things. He began to have dreams about the girl, whose thoughts made him happy, sitting as his pillion rider and both riding on a busy traffic.

"I am definitely going to ride the bike solo" said Haksh to himself, determined.

Another day Haksh was driving the bike in the field. Nabin was sitting pillion.

"You seem to be learning bike riding with such zeal. Any reason behind it?" asked Nabin.

"Because I want to learn."said Haksh

"But what will you do by learning bike riding?"

"Why?"

"You are wasting your time. You could use the Sundays in studying something"

"Brother, don't talk to me while I am riding the bike. I may lose my concentration and do something wrong. The bike may fall" Nabin did not say anything further.

After riding the bike for a long time in the field, Haksh headed towards the road.

"What are you doing? Why are you taking the bike on to the road ?" asked Nabin.

"I think I have been practising for a long time. Now, I should test my riding skills on the road" said Haksh. He took the bike **on to** the road. Haksh drove upto the daily market and headed towards home.

"I will tell father about this" said Nabin.

"What for?"asked Haksh.

"You have disobeyed him"

" Don't say like that. I did not disobey. If I do not ride on the road, how will I know my skills?"

Nabin entered the house and told his mother about Haksh riding the bike on the road.

"That's good. Haksh is beginning to take responsibilities. That shows he is maturing" said Mrs. Namita.

Haksh was overjoyed after hearing the words of his mother. Nabin was taken aback by this. He looked at Haksh.. After Mr. Bijay came, he made a decision that,Haksh would ride the bike on the road but under the supervision of Nabin.

Riding a bike makes the minds of youngsters fly. Haksh's mind began to fly when he realised the fact that he would now be riding the bike on the road. But he would always be under the watch of Nabin, he reminded himself. Haksh was planning to be free from any kind of observation.

His wish was granted.

One afternoon Haksh and Nabin were riding the bike.

"Mother had told to bring some vegetables. The vegetable shop was near our house but you wanted to ride the bike so you decided to come to the daily market"said Nabin.

"You got me brother" said Haksh.

"Get the vegetables and we will go home as soon as possible"

"But I have to tell you one thing"

"Yes"

"Can you give me half an hour to ride freely?"

"What?"

"It may sound odd but I want to ride with freedom. Brother, I have been riding the bike with you for a very long time so I want to test my skills alone"

Nabin told Haksh to halt the bike. Haksh obeyed.

Nabin got down and said "Haksh why do you want to ride the bike alone?"

"There is no reason. Just like that" said Haksh. "Just once **I would** like to ride the bike alone"

Haksh kept demanding to ride the bike solo. After a lot of persuading Nabin said ok.

"Come back to this place in thirty minutes. If you delay then I will tell Dad about you" said Nabin, giving an authoritative look at Haksh.

"Thank you brother." said Haksh. He started the bike and left the place. Haksh reached the daily market in five minutes and purchased the vegetables from a vegetable shop. He left the market.

"Time to show Chinmay, my riding skills" said Haksh to himself with a smile.

Haksh rode his bike into a lane and halted it outside a gate. He opened the hook of the gate and ran towards the house. He knocked the door. Chinmay opened the door.

"Haksh? You?" said Chinmay.

"I had told you that I would give you a ride on my bike, didn't I?" asked Haksh.

"Yes" said Chinmay.

"Come with me quickly. I have permission for some minutes only."

Chinmay told his mother that he would be back in fifteen minutes and left his home. Haksh drove the bike while Chinmay sat as the pillion rider.

"Where exactly are we going?" asked Chinmay.

"To the SSV school"

"Why are you going to my school?"

"Just like that. The road is nice" said Haksh and drove speedily.

The boys were nearing the school. There were some school children who were busy eating from the food stalls outside the school. A puddle of muddy water was on the road.

Haksh drove the bike on the puddle, resulting into muddy water being splashed on a girl, who was eating gupchup from a road side stall.

"Hey you!" shouted the girl from the stall.

"Oh no what have you done?" shouted Chinmay. "You splashed mud on that girl"

Haksh applied the brakes of his bike . " Really? I did that" said Haksh.

"Yes" said Chinmay.

"Let's escape" said Haksh. He turned his bike in front of the school and drove speedily.

The girl whose clothes had become muddy was looking at Haksh and Chinmay with anger. The boys left the place.

"Tomorrow I am going to have a very difficult day at school"said Chinmay.

"Why?"asked Haksh.

"The girl on whom the muddy water got splashed is my classmate"

"Will she shout at you?"

"No"

"Then ?"

"She will not speak to me"

"Then why to bother"

"You cannot understand"

"Why?"

"It's something that I cannot tell. You should not have done it. You should not have splashed water on the girl"

"What's her name? I will apologise to her"

"Elly"

"Okay if she shouts then tell her to meet me. I will apologise to her"

"That will come later. I will have to think of various ways to make her talk to me again"

"Why are you dying to talk to her?"

"You cannot understand my problem"

" I am getting a hint about it"

"What?"

"You are giving special attention to that girl"

"So?"

"You may be attracted towards her."

Haksh left Chinmay near at the latter's home and hurried towards his brother. Nabin was waiting at the place where Haksh had left him.

"You are late by five minutes" said Nabin.

"Oh so what? The traffic was busy"said Haksh. Nabin sat on the bike. The brothers returned home.

Chapter 5
Black liquid

* * *

AUGUST,2006
A BUSY ROAD OF PADAMPUR

Two girls were returning from the daily market. They were busy in their gossip. They were on foot with vegetable bags in their hands. One of them was in a pink frock and the other was in a frock that had a floral print on it. The girl in pink frock was the one who always sent Haksh dreaming whenever he saw her.

"I won't spare you?" came a shout .

SPLASH!

The girls closed their eyes and shouted in alarm. When they opened their eyes they found their frocks were stained in black paint.

"Oh no my dress!" said the girl in pink frock.

"My new dress!" said the other girl.

Both the girls looked at the trail of black paint sticking on the road and looked in the direction from which all this paint could have come. They found Haksh with a bucket in his hand. Haksh was standing there looking at the girls.

"Don't you have eyes!" shouted the girl who was in floral frock.

Haksh did not say anything. The girl in pink frock

gave an angry stare at him and walked away. **The** other girl followed. A boy walked upto Haksh and asked "What happened, Haksh?"

"Bhusan , why did you do it?" asked Haksh holding the collar of Bhusan.

Haksh was returning home after spending the day with friends. It was Sunday so he was in a mood to enjoy. While having fun with a friend he picked up a quarrel. Many times we find revelry turn into chaos when two people fight for no reason. Bhusan and Haksh were cracking jokes and other boys were listening when they began to tease each other. Haksh was growing fat so Bhusan was teasing him by calling him a buffalo. Haksh did not mind it initially but when the teasing went on , Haksh decided to bring an end to it and punched Bhusan. The latter ran to escape Haksh's anger. Haksh chased Bhusan. While chasing Bhusan, Haksh came across a mechanic's shop where bikes were being mended. Some boys of the mechanic shop knew Haksh. He borrowed a bucket that had black liquid in it.

"I will return it quickly" said Haksh and chased Bhusan. Vehicles were plying speedily on the road, so Bhusan had to halt. Haksh came close to him . Bhusan looked at him and said " Haksh, this is not good. You cannot stain my clothes . These are my new clothes"

" You called me buffalo. Let me make you as black as a buffalo" said Haksh and splashed the entire content of the bucket. Bhusan stepped aside. The liquid was splashed on him a bit , but missed a majority of his body . The two girls were walking on the road just behind Bhusan. The liquid got splashed on them. Haksh just stood there with a **blank expression** on his face. After the two girls left ,Haksh went to the mechanic shop and handed over the bucket to one of the grease monkeys. Bhusan saw Haksh who had no expression of anger on his face. Bhusan was happy that he **had** escaped Haksh's anger. He kept standing in his place till Haksh went out of sight .

Haksh was unable to eat at home as his mind was clouded by what had happened.He did not see the girl for several days, and he ultimately forgot about what had happened.

Chapter 6
Coaching centre

* * *

SEPTEMBER,2006
A COACHING CENTRE IN PADAMPUR

Haksh loved riding the bike whenever he got a chance. The rate at which he was riding the bike, Mr Bijay began to think he may have to purchase another bike because Haksh was always waiting for a chance to ride that bike.

One day Haksh went to Chinmay's home on his bike.

"Chinmay, let me drop you at your coaching centre today" said Haksh.

Chinmay was preparing to leave on his bicycle , but after getting the offer of Haksh, he left his bicycle and became Haksh's pillion rider.

Haksh drove upto a building and halted the bike. It was a two-storeyed building . The coaching classes were going on in the first floor. After Chinmay left, Haksh looked at the bicycles that had been parked outside the building. These bicycles belonged to the students who were inside the coaching centre. Haksh's attention was focussed on a Ladybird cycle. The sticker of a flower was stuck to the basket of the cycle.

" I think I have seen this cycle somewhere" said Haksh looking at the Ladybird cycle and trying to recall where he had seen it before.

"Where have I seen this bicycle ?" Haksh tried hard to recall.

Finally, he **succeeded** in recalling where he had seen the bicycle. He had seen the cycle when he was on his way to Barikel with his friends. A girl was riding it. It was the girl whom he saw wearing the pink frock in Mishra Babu's garden , the one who always left him charmed . Haksh smiled. He got down from his bike and walked upto the Ladybird bicycle. It was bright pink in colour. Haksh touched the bicycle and caressed its seat.

The coaching classes **went on** for an hour. He waited in front of the building for an hour . When the class was over, he returned to his bike. The students came out of the building. Chinmay walked upto Haksh. Haksh's eyes were not on Chinmay but on the girl whose thoughts always made him happy. The girl walked upto her bicycle, unlocked it and sat on it. She said goodbye to her friends and cycled away. Haksh kept looking at her. For some seconds he lost himself in his world of imagination where he saw himself riding the bike and the girl was sitting as his pillion rider.

" Haksh, let's go home" said Chinmay , putting his hand on **Haksh's** shoulder. Haksh came out of his world of imagination.

"Chinmay, I want to ask something" said Haksh.

"Yes, ask"

"What's the name of that girl?" asked Haksh pointing his finger at the girl riding the pink ladybird cycle . She had not yet gone out of sight.

Chinmay looked at the girl and said " That's Smrutisikha Meher. We call her Smruti"

"Smrutisikha Meher" said Haksh thoughtfully.

Chinmay felt Haksh's behaviour to be unusual. Haksh looked lost.

"What's the matter? Where are you lost?" asked

Chinmay.

"Nowhere" said Haksh coming out of his world of thoughts.

"There must be something. You are looking at her thoughtfully"

"I will tell you later. It's getting late." said Haksh. He sat on his bike and started it. The two friends left the place.

"Does this girl study with you at school ?" asked Haksh, while driving the bike

"Yes, she does" said Chinmay. "But why are you asking all this ?"

"Nothing"

Haksh left Chinmay at his home .

"Will you be coming tomorrow to give me a lift to my coaching centre ?" asked Chinmay.

" Do not depend on me. I may or may not be free always" said Haksh and left on his bike.

Haksh was glad to know the name of the girl whose thoughts had made him mad all these days. Her name was Smrutisikha Meher, in short Smruti.

Chapter 7
Maddened out

* * *

OCTOBER , 2006
PADAMPUR

"I will call her Smruti" said Haksh as he lay on his bed , looking at the ceiling.

He could not sleep properly the whole night out of joy. Haksh would always search for a chance to go to the Saraswati Sishu Vidyamandir school on his bike and keep waiting for the classes to be over. When the classes were over , the children would rush out of the school. Haksh would wait for Smruti.

Once Haksh spotted her, cycling her way on the road, he would keep standing and looking at her till she went out of sight. Once Smruti was out of sight , Haksh would leave the place. A time came when Haksh had to be serious about his lessons so he had to stop going to the school for some weeks. Smruti was again out of his mind.

JANUARY, 2007
A TRAFFIC CROSSING IN PADAMPUR

Smrutisikha was with her parents on an outing in a car. She was in the rear seat. Her father was driving the car. Due to heavy traffic, her father had to apply the brakes and halt the car . It was a traffic crossing. Once the traffic police showed green signal, Smrutisikha's father drove the car. Haksh who had halted his bike at the crossing saw Smruti and smiled. He followed the car on bike upto to some distance . He was maddened out of joy after seeing Smruti after a very long time.

Chapter 8
A change

* * *

JANUARY : 2007
PLACE: PADAMPUR

After knowing Smruti's name Haksh was always found smiling.

"Why are you smiling ?" asked Nabin to Haksh when he saw Haksh smiling.

"I am in a jolly mood" said Haksh.

"Any reason behind that ?"

"Nothing. The task given to me at school was easy, and I was able to complete it , so I am happy"

Nabin did not ask anything further.

The smile on Haksh's face was not something very negligible. For him it was like some sort of fulfilment or an accomplishment. A lot of changes had taken place in the behaviour of Haksh. He did not insist upon riding the bike. He seemed to be happy with his bicycle. He gave maximum time to his lessons.

The classes of Town High School were over by 4:15 pm in the afternoon. Haksh was always found around the school eating fast food from the local joints. This was a new habit that he had developed after getting into this school. A number of gupchup stalls had opened up near the school. Haksh began to eat more of fast food which deteriorated his health. The scenario changed when he was admitted in a coaching class. The tutor was one of his distant relatives. Other children also came to the same place to learn. He had to change one coaching centre and join another. This was his second coaching centre. His entry into the new coaching centre meant a lot **for** him. The time table which Haksh had made for him was no longer followed. He tore the timetable as it was of no use for him. He read whatever he liked and whenever he liked.

The coaching class for Haksh would start at 4:45 pm, Haksh did not have time to eat fast food anymore as he had to return home early and revise his lessons before going to the coaching classes. The memories of Smruti came to his mind but he had to deal with the heavy work load of his homework. He made a plan to make time for his lessons and have a glance of Smruti. After the classes were over at school , he would rush home and would leave on his bicycle. He did not eat his lunch. He would do all this in order to reach the entrance gate of the SSV school as early as possible. The boy would wait for the classes to be over at SSV. Once the classes were over, the children would come out from the school. Haksh would see Smruti cycling **her way home**.

Chapter 9
The mall

* * *

APRIL 2007
PADAMPUR

Haksh would smile at the sight of Smruti. He would follow the girl, but he would keep some distance from her so that no one could get a hint that he was following the girl. He would follow the girl upto some distance before heading towards his coaching centre. **He** would always make some time to see Smruti come out of her school.This went on till the annual examinations of class eighth came. Haksh cleared the exams.

The next academic session was going to start after a gap of a month or two. During this time Haksh attended coaching classes. Now, he was going to enter class nine which is the pre-board class. He could not take things lightly.

One afternoon, Chinmay came to meet Haksh. Both the friends greeted each other. They went to the courtyard of the house,where both of them began to talk over something.

"Haksh , have you visited the shopping mall that has recently opened in the town?"asked Chinmay.

"No" said Haksh. " Shopping malls are for rich people. I have no work there"

" But you should pay a visit to it"

"What for?"

"It is fantastic ! I'm going there today. I want you to join me ."

"I have no work there, so why should I go there ?" said Haksh.

"I need your help. Once you reach there, you will know why I called you ," said Chinmay.

"Okay, I will come"

"Thank you"

"But we will go on bicycle. My brother has not yet returned from college .There is no bike at home,"said Haksh.

Both the boys left for the mall on their bicycles. While riding the cycle Haksh looked at Chinmay. He was constantly looking at his watch.

"Why are you looking at the wrist watch so much?"asked Haksh.

"Just ride speedily ," said Chinmay.

Haksh followed Chinmay. The latter halted outside the shopping mall.

"Have you got any money with you?" asked Chinmay to Haksh.

"Why?' asked Haksh.

"Suppose we find something we can purchase" said Chinmay.

"You should have told that to me earlier. I have only a hundred rupee note with me"

Chinmay scratched his head thoughtfully.

"I can help you ," said Haksh. " You wait here . I am coming"

Haksh rode his bicycle and left the mall. He entered the colony that was near the shopping mall. He halted near a house and got down from his cycle. He opened the hook of the gate and went to the front door of the house. The house belonged to Alok,a friend of Haksh. Haksh met Alok and told him to come to the shopping mall. Alok took out his bicycle and went to the shopping mall with Haksh. Chinmay was waiting for them. The three boys entered the shopping mall.

"What are you going to purchase? I have come with a five hundred rupee note" said Alok.

" Let us see the whole mall, then we will think about purchasing" said Haksh.

While moving around in the mall , Haksh observed Chinmay's behaviour. Chinmay was not paying attention to the various stalls in the mall. His attention was more towards the people moving about inside the mall.He put his hand on the back of Chinmay ,saying, "Chinmay, I have to ask you something"

"Yes" said Chinmay, startled.

" Have you really come here for shopping or for anything else ?".

Chinmay tried to hide his intentions, but Haksh was adamant to know about what was in Chinmay's mind. Finally, Chinmay spoke what he was hiding in his mind.That day at the coaching centre , he had heard Elly talk with Smruti. Both the girls were planning to go to the shopping mall .

" I see. So you are here to see Elly" said Haksh.

"We have been roaming about in the mall for a long time. When are we going to purchase anything?"asked Alok.

"Be patient , my friend" said Haksh.

Haksh and Chinmay began to search for Elly and Smruti.

"If we move like this , the security personnel will think us to be thieves. Let us buy something" said Haksh.

Chinmay looked at a stall that sold gifts.

"Let us purchase some gifts" said Chinmay.

The three boys entered the gift shop and began to see what they could purchase. The stall had walls made up of glass. Haksh was looking outside the shop through the glass. He saw Smruti going up in a lift. The mall had lift system in order to help customers go to the shops that were on the third floor of the mall. Haksh came out of the gift shop in order to see whether it was Smruti or not.

The lift halted at the third floor. Haksh used the stairs and reached the third floor. He stood some feet away from the entrance of the lift.The door opened and two girls came out with a middle aged couple.

Smruti was talking with the middle aged couple. The girl with her was walking silently.

" That couple must be Smruti's parents. The girl with Smruti must be Elly" said Haksh in a low voice.

He ran to the gift shop in the second floor and informed Chinmay about Smruti's arrival.

"Elly must be with Smruti" said Chinmay.

"Can anyone tell me what's going on?" asked Alok.

"Alok, you just give us half an hour. Just wait outside the mall. We will be joining you" said Haksh to Alok.

Alok left the shop and headed towards the exit of the shopping mall.

"Where did you see them?" asked Chinmay.

"Come with me" said Haksh.

The two boys left the gift shop and went to the third floor. All the shops in the mall had walls made up of glass. They saw Smruti and Elly in a dress shop.

"Oh, no !" said Chinmay.

"What happened ?" asked Haksh.

" Smruti's parents are there" said Chinmay.

"So what?"

"I am leaving" said Chinmay.

"But you wanted to see Elly for some time?"

" I saw her. My objective is complete. Now, I must leave" said Chinmay and left.

Haksh did not go. He stayed in the mall looking at Smruti through the **glass-wall** from outside the shop. Smruti was looking at various dresses available in the shop. She chose a dress and called her mother. The mother and the daughter discussed on the dress.

" Smruti wants a dress" said Haksh , observing the activities of Smruti.

Smruti and her parents stood near the counter with the dress chosen by Smruti. Elly was yet to purchase **something** . She was just looking at the variety of dresses in the mall. Smruti called her.

Elly walked upto her. Smruti's father made payment for the dress.

"It's time to leave before these girls spot me" said Haksh and walked away.

Smruti , her parents and Elly entered another shop. This was a jewellery shop. Haksh stood outside the shop and looked at the activities of Smruti through the glass wall of the shop. Smruti and Elly were looking at necklaces and pendants with a lot of enthusiasm. Smruti chose a pendent with red stone and Elly chose a necklace.

"So you like red stones" said Haksh, looking at Smruti.

Haksh knew they would be coming out of the shop at anytime so he left the place. The family went to the lift and enterd it. They reached the ground floor. Haksh kept an eye on them from the third floor. The girls entered a fast food stall. Smruti's parents followed them.

"Time to eat some fast food" said Haksh and entered the lift. He reached the ground floor and entered the fast food stall. The fast food stall was crowded inside. Haksh looked at Smruti and Elly. Both of them were eating two big pieces of cake . **From the** speed at which the girls were eating the cake, it appeared as if they had not eaten for days. Both of them consumed their **pieces** of cake and asked for some more big slices of cake. Smruti's parents were eating two dosas. Haksh wanted to eat something. His mouth was **salivating** . The boy took out a five hundred rupee note **from** his pant pocket.

One may be thinking how he got the money. Well, Alok had got the money . He gave it to Chinmay. Chinmay was purchasing a gift in the gift shop when Haksh informed him about Smruti and Elly. Chinmay was excited about it. He did not buy the gift and decided to follow Smruti and Elly. Haksh told Alok to leave. When Chinmay wanted to leave the mall, Haksh took the money from him promising him that he would get something for Chinmay.

In the fast food stall, Haksh decided to eat some chowmein.

" Two plates of chowmein" said Haksh.

The man who was making fast food gave him food. Haksh ate it . He asked for one more plateful of it. The man gave another plate. The boy ate that plate of chowmein. While eating the chowmein, he forgot all about Smruti and Elly, who were eating another piece of cake. After finishing plates of chowmein, Haksh paid the bill. After paying the bill, he looked at the chairs that had been occupied by Elly and Smruti. The two girls were about to leave.

"Time to leave" said Haksh. He left the food stall before the girls could.

Smruti, her parents and Elly went to the exit and left the shopping mall. Haksh saw them leave. He remained in the mall as he had to purchase something. He bought the gift which Chinmay wanted to purchase. The boy left the mall. By the time he left it was dark. Haksh looked at the night sky and realized the amount of time he had spent in the mall.A car passed in front of him . Haksh saw the girl in the back seat of the car. It was Smruti.

Haksh cycled his way home. He knocked **at** the door . Nabin opened it.

" Where were you ?" asked Nabin.

"Mother must have told you" said Haksh.

"What is that decorative card doing in your hand?"

"That's my friend's . He told me to get it for him"

"Chinmay left you alone in the mall **?** "

"This was the first time I was in the mall , so I spent

a lot of time in it"

"What's the matter Nabin?" said Namita. "Stop becoming a policeman. He had gone to the mall"

"Nabin seems to be a policeman in the making" said Mr.Bijay.

Chapter 10
Hardworking student

* * *

JULY, 2007
PLACE: PADAMPUR

A new day started. The wind was blowing gently due to some melancholy in the Bay of Bengal. We do not have gentle wind blowing in the scorching summers. The sky was **overcast** and there was a heavy downpour. Haksh was lying on his bed and was changing sides from time to time. Like every day, he had Smruti's name on his lips.

"What must Smruti be doing **at** her home to spend **the** time? Wow. She must be living a beautiful life in her house. Her father must be very rich and she must be living the life of a princess. Oooo Smruti" said Haksh pressing the pillow in his arms and kissing it. When in love, people begin to imagine a number of things.

Haksh opened his eyes. In front of him was the wall against which there was his bed. On the wall was written in pencil "Smruti". Haksh smiled on seeing the writing on the wall. It was written in pencil.

"Good morning Smruti" said Haksh with a smile on his face. He was given a room as he had entered the pre-board class. He was given a room so that he is not disturbed by others. Haksh was thinking a lot about Smruti, so let us learn something about Smruti.

The alarm clock went off, a hand crawled out from under the bed sheet and slapped the top of the clock that was kept on the **side table**. The clock stopped. The hand removed the bed sheet and we had Smruti lying on her bed. Her sleep had just broken. She twisted her limbs for sometime before sitting up on the bed and giving a loud yawn. She looked at the **wall clock**.

"Hmmm..." she said after looking at the time. The next thing she did was looking at the date on the calendar that was hanging from the wall. She scratched her head and left the bed. She went to the

wash basin and opened the tap. She washed her face and returned to her room. She looked at the **calendar** one more time.

"So ,there is class test today" she said to herself. "No problem. I have just to revise my lessons"

"Smruti have your bath and eat your breakfast" her mother shouted.

"Cover my food, Maa. I'll have my breakfast after completing my revision for my class test" said Smruti.

This was Smruti- a hardworking student . She had an elder brother who was studying in **a** college.

Smruti completed the revision of her lessons and got ready to face the class test at school. She left home on her bicycle.

At school, she did not talk to anyone until the class test was over. After the classes were over ,Smruti left the school on her bicycle. She was cycling comfortably with a smile on her face. She must have done well in the class test.

"Hey Smruti" Smruti heard someone call her. She looked to her right. She found her classmate Binita on a cycle. Binita was cycling close to Smruti.

"How much will you score in the class test?" asked Binita.

"Some twenty-five or twenty-eight out of thirty" said

Smruti.

"Why are you not so confident over your marks?"asked Binita. "You are a very intelligent girl"

"Don't patronize me" said Smruti.

"I am not patronizing. I am just telling you the truth. I **wish I** could be as studious as you."

"Why?"

"Because of my below average and sometimes just-average marks I get a lot of scolding at home. My parents take my studies so seriously that I never get any free time to play or for any entertainment. Whenever I am found watching some movie or any serial on the t.v., I am shouted at and sent to my room. I have to watch the t.v. stealthily. Good marks bring a lot of freedom to a person"

Haksh was standing on the side of the road. He was waiting for Smruti. Smruti and Binita crossed before him on the road. Haksh was elated to see Smruti.

Binita departerd and Smruti was cycling alone. Haksh followed the girl for some distance then stopped following her. He overtook her. While overtaking Smruti, he looked at her face. Smruti's eyes fell on the Haksh, who was looking at her.

"I see this boy around me almost everyday. He just keeps looking at me. This boy blackened my dress the other day" thought Smruti. "Who is this boy? What does he want?" She kept thinking.

Haksh was cycling speedily. He disappeared from Smruti's sight.

"But why am I thinking about this boy. He must be like other roadside rustic guys with low character who just keep looking at girls" said Smruti to herself. She shook her head a bit from side to side as if to remove the thoughts of Haksh from her mind and kept cycling towards her home.

SEPTEMBER, 2007
AT COACHING CENTRE

One day the teacher who was coaching Haksh and other students wanted to meet all his students. All the students gathered in front of the teacher.

"Students I have called you here to say that I am going to stop teaching children as I have to prepare for a competitive examination" said the teacher.

"But why do you have to suspend the coaching now, Sir? We are in the pre-board class. We have been performing well in our exams only because of you. If you stop teaching us then we will have no hope of getting good marks in examinations" said Haksh.

The boy was trying to persuade the teacher to change his mind and resume teaching children. The other children present in the classroom had the same **thing** to say.

"Children" said the teacher raising his hands. They all went silent. "I understand your problem, but I want to tell you my problem. You want me to teach you. You want me to teach you upto the end of the board exams of class ten ,right?"

"Yes" said the students in chorus.

"If that is the case then let me tell you about my problem. The competitive exam is going to help me get a good job. If I score good marks in the exam, I will get a good job. In order to score good marks, I have to prepare well. Do you want to be the reason behind my disqualification in getting the job?" said the teacher

The students were speechless. They began to look at each other with blank faces. Nobody understood what was to be said. They could feel the intensity in the room.

"If that's the case" said Haksh standing up from the bench. "We are ready to stop coming to you for classes. We will allow you to prepare well for the exam"

The students decided to terminate the coaching

classes in order to allow the teacher prepare for competitive examinations. A farewell was arranged. **The children** who came to the coaching centre arranged a feast.

"Thank you students. Thank you for the farewell" said the teacher.

Haksh appeared **to be** happy, but in his mind he was worried. Now, his father will have to arrange a new coaching teacher for him. Mr. Bijay had to do something for his son in order to prepare him for the board exams.

OCTOBER , 2007
PADAMPUR

One afternoon, Bijay told Haksh to come with him. It was a Monday afternoon. Haksh had come back from his school classes.

Bijay said "I am taking you to the place where you are going to take your coaching classes hereafter"

"Really?" said Haksh.

"Yes"

"I was really worried about my preparations for my exam"

Bijay took Haksh to the new coaching centre on his bike. The way to the coaching centre looked familiar to Haksh. Bijay halted his bike near a two storeyed building and told Haksh to get down from the bike. Haksh knew the place. It was the coaching centre where Chinmay used to come to study.

"Your next teacher will be Sir Jiten" said Mr Bijay.

Bijay and Haksh got down **from** the bike. Bijay rang up Jiten who was busy teaching children in the coaching centre.

"Sir I am waiting for **you** outside your **coaching** centre" said Mr. Bijay before ending his conversation. He looked at Haksh and said "Be here while I have a chat with Jiten about your coaching fees and **other things**"

Haksh stood near the bike and looked at the building. There was a huge grin on his face because it was the same building where Smruti came for coaching.

"Never knew that fate had such a big surprise in store for me?" thought Haksh. "It is very difficult to believe that I am going to study in the same coaching centre where Smruti comes to study. Thank you God"

Haksh kept looking at the building forgetting the world. He kept looking at the coaching centre until he felt a hand on his right shoulder. Haksh looked to his right and found Sir Jiten standing near him.

"Are you worried, son.?" asked Sir Jiten looking at Haksh. He did not say anything. He was unable to understand what to say.

"Don't worry. I will help you in your studies" said Sir Jiten.

He took Haksh into the coaching centre. The coaching centre of Sir Jiten was in the upper floor of the two-storeyed building. Haksh entered the coaching centre. There were some sixteen children in the room of the coaching centre. The seating arrangement of the children was in the form of a crescent moon. All of them were looking at the blackboard infront of them. Something was written on the blackboard. Haksh entered the classroom. He was told to sit near the door of the classroom. Sir Jiten introduced Haksh to the rest of the students present in the classroom. Sir Jiten stood infront of the kids and called Haksh. He stood up from the floor and walked upto Sir Jiten.

"Hello children," said Sir Jiten.

All the children looked at Sir Jiten.

"We have a new student with us" said the teacher and put his hand on the shoulder of Haksh. "His name is Haksh" added the teacher.

The students did not say anything. They just kept looking at Haksh. He was not feeling the surrounding to be new as he had some of his friends like Chinmay, in the room.

"You can go back to your place, son," said Sir Jiten.

Haksh returned to his place of sitting. Haksh was not looking happy. When Sir Jiten began to write something on the blackboard, Haksh looked at the faces of the children who were studying with him.

"Where's that girl?" thought Haksh while looking at the children."Where is Smruti?"

It did not take much time for him to locate her. She was sitting in the far end near the wall that was opposite to the door. She was wearing a scarf because of which Haksh was unable to spot her initially.

When she removed her scarf, Haksh could recognise her. She was in a pastel blue frock. Her eyes were only on the blackboard. The sight of Smruti made Haksh feel as if he was the luckiest person on the planet. The coaching class went on for forty-five minutes. Haksh looked at Smruti's face the whole time. By the time he was back home, he had a very wide smile on his face. After the classes at school ended, he would rush to **his** coaching classes on time. Haksh would do all the given homework on time and score good marks in tests. Haksh was doing all this to attract the attention of the students **studying** with him in his batch in the coaching centre. Smruti had seen him before, so she was not giving any importance to his presence. She always gave priority to her lessons. Haksh always looked at Smruti's face in the coaching centre, while Smruti focussed on the blackboard.

NOVEMBER, 2007
PADAMPUR

After getting the luck of studying with Smruti in the same coaching centre, Haksh was feeling the want to spend more time with her. He was very punctual in attending the coaching classes of Sir Jiten. Once inside the coaching class, he would spend most of the time looking at the face of Smruti.

The days on which Smruti did not come to the coaching class would become very difficult for Haksh to spend in the coaching class. The day he could not see Smruti made him restless. The time table of Haksh changed. Everyday, he reached home on bicycle after his classes were over at school and have lunch as fast as he could. After lunch, he would cycle upto Saraswati Sishu Vidyamandir and halt there. Smruti would come out of the school on her cycle. Haksh would follow her on cycle. After following the girl for some distance Haksh would follow a different route to the coaching centre of Sir Jiten. Smruti would head to her home before coming to the coaching centre. At the coaching centre, Haksh would stand near the building where the coaching classes were held and wait for Smruti. After school, Smruti would go home to change her uniform and wear something causal. She would eat some snacks before coming to Sir Jiten. Whenever Smruti reached the coaching centere, Haksh would be delighted at her sight. The boy would enter the coaching centre after the girl came.

As days passed, Haksh became more adventurous. He began to follow Smruti after the coaching classes were over. Haksh was curious to know where Smruti lived. He followed her by keeping sufficient distance from her. Smruti would halt infront of her house. Haksh would halt several meters away from her. He would watch Smruti enter her house .Once the girl entered the house the boy left the place. This became a routine for him on all working days. Haksh was happy that he was following the girl everyday upto her home and Smruti had no problem because she **never** marked Haksh following her. She was very serious over her lessons, so she did not have time to think whether anyone followed her or not. One day while looking at the blackboard and copying down whatever was being written on the blackboard, Smruti caught sight of Haksh. The latter was looking at her and smiling. She did not give any importance to it. As time passed she **found** Haksh following her after the classes were over at school and after the classes were over at the coaching centre.

"Well, it was okay if the boy wanted to study in the coaching centre to which I go, but he is following me a lot. He keeps looking at me at the coaching centre . He is even following me to my home now. I will complain to my parents if he crosses the limit or does any kind of nuisance" thought Smruti when she saw Haksh following her one day.

Haksh knew Smruti had noticed his activites, but instead of being afraid of any action from Smruti's side, he was happy that Smruti was noticing him whenever he was near her.

Elly studied in the coaching centre of Sir Jiten. Chinmay was always careful in dealing with her. He never tired to hurt Elly. Haksh knew Chinmay liked Elly.

"Have you told Elly that you like her?"asked Haksh.

"Yes, she knows it" said Chinmay.

"You are lucky. In my case, I do not enjoy that luck"

"Means?"

"I have not told my girl that I love her"

"Are you talking about Smruti?"

"Yes"

The two boys were talking while coming back from the coaching centre. Haksh did not follow Smruti that day.

"I knew you had something in your mind about Smruti" said Chinmay.

"She has been looking at me for **some time**. But how to make her know that I love her?" asked Haksh.

"Very simple"

"How?"

"Write a love letter"

"What?" Haksh was taken aback. "I have never written any such thing in my whole life"

"You had never fallen in love until Smruti came into your life"

"You are right"

"Try to write one. Just take out a plain sheet of paper and write whatever you feel about Smruti"

"Okay"

That day after returning from the coaching centre, Haksh sat at his study table. In front of him was a plain sheet of paper with a pen lying on it. Haksh was looking at the sheet of paper and thinking. After a lot of thinking, Haksh realised he could not write any love letter. He was left sad about it. Haksh was not illiterate. He was good at English but he was restrained due to the fear of the consequences. Writing a love letter and giving it to a girl could be hazardous. You are never sure about the response that will come. The girl might accept **it** but what if she rejects it and calls her parents to deal with the situation.

"Should I write it or not" thought Haksh. After thinking for a long time he came up with a plan.

Nabin was a college student now. One morning Haksh called Nabin when the latter was about to leave home in order to go to college. Haksh had often seen Nabin smiling a lot for no reason. He felt as if Nabin was having some affair with some girl in the college.

"What's the matter?" asked Nabin.

"One of my friends is in love with a girl but he is unable to express it. He wants to write a letter to that girl . **What** should he write **?** Can you help me?" asked Haksh.

"Is it your friend or it's you who's in love?" asked Nabin.

"Me ? Never. I have the board exams coming"

"Never do that thing. It will waste your time"

"It's my friend"

"Bring me a paper. I will write it."

Haksh went to his room and came with a piece of paper and a pen. Nabin wrote something and handed it over to Haksh.

"Never do anything which could destroy your career" said Nabin and left.

Haksh was going to leave home after some minutes. He rushed to his room with joy. Haksh opened the piece of paper to read **it**. The content in the letter was "I love you but I've no courage to tell you".Haksh folded the paper and put it in his school bag.

After school, Haksh rushed to the coaching centre. He stood outside the coaching centre and waited for the rest of his batch mates. The children came on their bicycles and entered the coaching centre. Haksh saw Smruti and smiled. After all the children had entered the coaching centre, Haksh took out the piece of paper from his bag and put it in the basket fitted to the handle of Smruti's Ladybird cycle.

"Whatever happens will be seen" said Haksh and entered the coaching centre.

After the coaching classes were over, Haksh headed straight to his home. Haksh could not read anything at home. The boy had given the letter to the girl but he had not written his name, so it was not going to be easy for Smruti to know the identity of the sender. The purpose of the letter was to make Smruti know someone is in love with her.

"Tomorrow she will surelly try to ask her friend about it. She will be surprised over the whole matter" said Haksh.

The next day when Haksh went to the coaching centre, he did not look at Smruti. From the time Haksh entered the coaching centre till the time he left the place, Haksh was expecting Smruti to do some inquiry about the love letter. Smruti did not ask anyone about the love letter. She behaved as if nothing had happened. Smruti's behaviour puzzled Haksh. He waited for a week just to see if the letter had made Smruti show some reaction, but the girl did not even enquire anyone about it.

So, what happened to the letter ?

That day after reaching home, Smruti saw the letter. She read the content, shrugged her shoulders and threw it.

"May be someone had put it in my basket by mistake" said Smruti and threw it in the dust bin.

NOVEMBER, 2007
A FAST FOOD STALL IN PADAMPUR

"This is very strange" said Haksh to Chinmay when both were eating at a fast food stall one Sunday.

"What is strange?" asked Chinmay.

"I gave the letter, but she did not give any reaction"

"What were you expecting from her?"

"I expected her to ask her friends if anyone had tried to give any letter to her"

"Oh"

"But she did not even ask anyone about it"

"This is very strange"

"Did she even read it or not ?"

"We cannot say? From the way she is reacting, I don't think she might have read it"

"What to do now?"

"What if you give a letter to her directly ?"

"What?" Haksh was taken aback.

"Just chill. It is just a suggestion" said Chinmay.

"I will think about it"

After getting no response from Smruti, Haksh felt a bit disappointed.

After having a discussion with Chinmay, he made a plan to speak directly to Smruti.

"I will halt her by bringing my bicycle infront of her bicycle" said Haksh.

"Then what will you tell her ?" asked Chinmay.

"I will say 'I have to say something to you'" said Haksh.

"Then?" asked Chinmay.

"I will tell her I love her" said Haksh.

"You will need a lot of courage to do that"

Haksh began to practice at home. He would think of various ways of telling what he felt about Smruti. It is always difficult for a boy to tell a girl about what he feels for her.

NOVEMBER, 2007
A ROAD IN PADAMPUR

One day after the coaching classes were over, Haksh followed Smruti on his bicycle. The boy was feeling as if he was going to do something great. He was clearly nervous but he wanted to go ahead with the plan. This was the first time that he was going to make an attempt to propose someone directly.

Smruti was cycling slowly. She reached the lane in which her house was located. Haksh sped up and came close to Smruti. He overtook her and stopped his bicycle infront of Smruti. Smruti had to apply sudden brakes in order to bring her bicycle to a halt.

"I have to say something" said Haksh.

Smruti looked at Haksh, sharply. The boy looked at her. She kept gazing at Haksh. He could not say anything further. The previous night Haksh had practiced a lot on how he would speak to Smruti, but now all his practice went in vain. He was overcome by a mental block because of the Smruti's gaze .

The girl looked at Haksh for few more seconds then looked at the road. She turned the handle of her bicycle and headed towards her home. Haksh stood at his place, looking at Smruti leave.

NOVEMBER, 2007
A PARK IN PADAMPUR

"What!! You could not say anything even after coming infront of her !" exclaimed Chinmay after Haksh told him about that incident with Smruti.

It was again a Sunday and the two friends were walking in a park.

"I don't know what went wrong with me. I stopped her but could not say anything further to her. I just don't understand what just happened to me when I made a direct eye to eye contact with her" said Haksh in disappointment. Both of them were sitting on the steps of a temple located near the park.

"Such things happen, buddy" said a sympathetic Chinmay, patting the back of the Haksh. "This was your first attempt so you might have felt a mental block"

"Yes, you are right"

"Hmmm..."

"It seems I can never tell her about my love"

"Don't be so sad. You will tell her about your love one day"

Haksh could not forget the way he stopped Smruti on the way and how he had failed to tell her about his love.

"I could have told her. My mind just went blank" said Haksh to himself in his room.

NOVEMBER, 2007

THE COACHING CENTRE OF SIR JITEN

Haksh kept going to the coaching centre but he did not look at Smruti as he used to do before. He did not follow the girl anymore.

Did that mean he had given up? No, not at all. He was busy planning a surprise for Smruti.

Smruti had not told anyone about the way Haksh had halted her on the road. This was something peculiar about her. She did not want to entangle herself in anything.

JANUARY,2008

A LANE IN PADAMPUR

It was another day of the coaching centre for the

students going to the coaching centre of Sir Jiten. When the coaching classes were over, Haksh followed the cycle-borne Smruti. When both of them reached the lane where Smruti's house was located, Haksh sped up a bit and halted his bicycle deliberately in front of Smruti's bicycle. Smruti had to apply brakes on her cycle and halt. Haksh pushed his hand into his pant pocket. He took out a piece of paper from it and put the paper into the basket that was fitted to the handle of Smruti's Ladybird cycle. He did not halt. He rode his bicycle and fled. Smruti kept looking at the boy. She was confused about what just happened in front of her.

JANUARY, 2008
IN THE ROOM OF HAKSH

Haksh was restless the whole day. He was getting prepared for the worst thing. He was anticipating Smruti trying to get him punished with the help of her parents.

"Smruti would tell Sir Jiten about the letter. Sir may tell my father about it" thought Haksh.

JANUARY, 2008
AT THE COACHING CENTRE

The next day at the coaching centre, Haksh did not look at Smruti. He was expecting Smruti to complain against him, but nothing of that sort took place. Smruti looked at Haksh with anger. Haksh marked it. He did not follow her anymore. He felt bad about himself.

"I've hurt her so much. I should not have done it" thought Haksh and wanted to apologise. He told Chinmay about it.

"Never think about that" said Chinmay.

Haksh did not apologise to Smruti. He did not follow her anymore. As time passed Haksh's friends came to know about the love Haksh had for Smruti. Even the boys who were the batchmates of Haksh in Sir Jiten's coaching centre came to know about the one-sided love that Haksh had for Smruti.

How did this take place?

All of them had seen Haksh follow Smruti a number of times , **but** for some weeks they did not see Haksh anywhere near Smruti which made them feel there was something between Haksh and Smruti.

"Go and propose the girl" said a boy to Haksh when the latter was walking out of the coaching centre.

That day after the coaching class was over, the boys who were the batch mates of Haksh in the coaching centre surrounded him and asked if he had any problem in his affair with Smruti. They wanted to help Haksh in his love affair.

"I have already given her a love letter, but she shows no reaction. She is neither complaining to anyone about it nor is she smiling at me." said Haksh.

"Don't worry. Your love is sincere, because you are missing her" said another boy.

" Don't feel dejected. We will support you" spoke one more boy.

Before the boys left Haksh, they made a decision. The decision was that every day some boy or the other from the batch of boys, who went to sir Jiten as batch mates of Haksh , would give a love letter

and a chocolate to Haksh. Haksh was supposed to put that love letter in the basket fitted to the handle of Smruti's bicycle.

Chapter 11
The detention

* * *

JANUARY, 2008
AT THE COACHING CENTRE

Haksh took the letters and the chocolates but he thought several times before proceeding to give them to Smruti. He would follow Smruti after the end of the coaching classes. It would be proper to say he was compelled to follow the girl by his friends because Haksh had no interest in following the girl anymore. There might be some fear in his mind.

Haksh would follow the girl but only for a short distance, then he would head towards his home. At home he entered his room and ate the chocolates that he was supposed to give to Smruti. He read the letters and put them in an old school bag that was not in use anymore.

"I feel as if I am experiencing some sort of ragging because I am in love with some girl" said Haksh to himself when he thought of the way his friends were forcing him to give the love letters and the chocolates to Smruti. If anyone ever asked him about the letters and the chocolates, Haksh would lie by telling them he gave them to Smruti. If anyone asked about Smruti's reaction after getting the letters and the chocolates, Haksh would lie to them. Sometimes he would say Smruti smiled and sometimes he would say Smruti did not show any reaction. Lying is not a virtue, but sometimes it brings you sweet things. Haksh's friends gave him chocolates and told him to give them to Smruti.

The chocolates were not cheap chocolates. They were Cadbury dairy milk chocolate bars, Kitkat chocolate bars, Nestle Milky bars and sometimes Amul chocolate bars. Haksh ate all these chocolates at home. Why shouldn't he when he was getting them at free of cost? So, Haksh was having some kind **of** benefit from his love affair with Smruti.

Haksh was enjoying eating the chocolates. More surprises were waiting for him. One day Sir Jiten detained him at the coaching centre after the coaching class for the day was over. Haksh was wondering why he was detained. Sir Jiten sat on a chair in the room and called him to stand near him.

"Are you in love with Smruti?" asked Sir Jiten.

Haksh was taken aback.

"Tell the truth" said Sir Jiten.

"That girl must have told sir about my activites" thought Haksh.

"Yes....sir...no ....sir..." Haksh answered, fumbling. He was afraid.

"Be easy, kid. I have been observing your behaviour for some days. You have your eyes on Smruti. You always look at her" said Sir Jiten. Haksh did not say anything. He did not understand what to say.

"It's okay if you love her, but give importance to your lessons. Don't let your mind fly. Your career is important for you."spoke the teacher.

"I will sir" said Haksh with his head lowered.

"You have to" said Sir Jiten and let Haksh leave the room.

Haksh did not know what to do. He loved Smruti but he was afraid to do any further advances towards her. Now, the teacher had come to know about his love affair which meant he would have to do well in the tests **at** the coaching centre. Till that day he had never thought so much about his academic career, because he thought he had scored good marks in the past, he was scoring good marks in the present and he will be scoring good marks in the future. Sir Jiten's words made him think.

Chapter 12
Romantic drives

* * *

SEPTEMBER, 2008
PADAMPUR

The annual exams of class ninth came. Haksh cleared them and entered class ten, the board class. He was going to face his first public examination. The entry to class tenth brought in some changes in Haksh's habits. The academic session of class tenth started in the month of April. Haksh kept going to the coaching class of Sir Jiten. The boy was busy in preparing for the half-yearly examinations that would precede the board examinations of class ten. A few months before the half yearly **examinations** could begin, Haksh found his friends Chinmay, Sumit and Ajay had left the coaching centre of Sir Jiten and joined the coaching centre of a tutor named Ramesh.

Ramesh was again another relative of Mr Bijay. When Haksh found three of his friends had left Sir Jiten's coaching centre, he too decided to leave the coaching centre of sir Jiten. He had another reason behind this decision. The reason was Smruti. Haksh had become fed up with his own love life. Sir Jiten's words had made him thoughtful about his career. The boy made up his mind and decided to stress on his career and stop thinking about Smruti . **It** is not so easy to execute whatever you think in the mind. Whenever he went to the coaching centre his eyes went to Smruti, who came to the coaching centre even after knowing about Haksh's activities. Smruti would always invoke the lover in Haksh. The boy wanted to leave the coaching centre, so that he would not see Smruti again.

Haksh changed his coaching centre. He stopped going to Sir Jiten. Now, he went to Sir Ramesh. Smruti was nowhere around in the new coaching centre, so he was not having any romantic drives anymore. A month passed, Haksh was working very hard with his lessons and preparing to do very well in the exams.

OCTOBER, 2008
A COACHING CENTRE IN PADAMPUR

One day Sir Ramesh entered the classroom and said "Students today we have a new student joining us"

The students in the classroom were curious to see the new student.

"The new student's name is Smruti" said Sir Ramesh.

Smruti entered the room. Haksh's eyes were left wide open when he saw Smruti enter the room.

"Congratulations,Haksh" whispered Chinmay to Haksh. "Fate has once again brought her close to you"

Haksh had a very wide smile on his face. He felt as if he had found something **which** he had lost long ago. Even if he wanted to be away from her to focus on his lessons, he could not forget her completely.

The boy was happy to see Smruti **at** the coaching centre of Sir Ramesh, but he could not look at her in the way he used to look at her in the coaching centre of Sir Jiten because there was the fear of Sir Ramesh telling his father about it.

Every day after the coaching classes of Sir Ramesh were over Haksh would go to his cycle. After reaching his bicycle, he would stand near the cycle and look at Smruti's

Ladybird cycle. The girl would go to her cycle, unlock it , sit on the seat and cycle away. The boy would enjoy the sight of Smruti cycling away.

Chapter 13
The innocence

* * *

MAY, 2008

A COACHING CENTRE

One day after the coaching classes were over and Haksh was busy watching Smruti unlock her cycle and paddle it, he heard a voice ask "Haksh did you enjoy watching Smruti cycle?"

Haksh looked to his left and found Chinmay standing near him.

"Yes" said Haksh. "But why?" asked Haksh

"Let all the students leave" said Chinmay.

All the boys and girls left the coaching centre. Haksh and Chinmay stood outside the coaching centre.

"Now say what's the matter?" asked Haksh.

Punch!

Chinmay punched Haksh. The latter was taken aback. Chinmay rained a few more blows on Haksh's face.

"It's for you that Elly is not talking to me anymore. You created the misunderstanding between Elly and me" said an angry Chinmay while raining punches on Haksh's face.

After punching Haksh for sometime Chinmay took some rest. He was fuming in rage.

"Are you done?" asked Haksh, pressing his right hand on his right cheek . That cheek was paining a lot.

Chinmay did not say anything.

"I have not done anything. I have not done anything to create any misunderstanding between you and Elly. The day you realise it, you will feel sorry for punching me today."

For some days a misunderstanding had been going on between Elly and Chinmay. Elly had stopped talking to Chinmay for some reason and had started to hate him. The culprit behind this was a boy who wanted Elly to be his. That boy used to say various bad things about Chinmay to Elly in order to make Elly hate Chinmay. The boy's name was Umesh.

Umesh would tell Elly that he had collected all kinds of information about Chinmay being a bad boy. He said he had got this information from Haksh, Chinmay's best friend. Elly believed in Umesh and did not behave properly with Chinmay. When Chinmay asked Elly what had happened to her, the girl told him that she had come to know everything about his bad habits from Haksh. Chinmay was taken aback at this . **From** that day he nurtured a grudge against Haksh. It was out of rage that he beat Haksh.

As you know any kind of lie cannot hide for long. Chinmay soon discovered Haksh's innocence and felt sorry for beating the latter. Haksh forgave Chinmay and said "I never felt bad about you. I was waiting for the day you realised your mistake"

The two friends embraced each other.

JANUARY, 2009
A VILLAGE IN PADAMPUR

Mr Bijay wanted to shift his house to his village. A change in house meant Haksh would have to change his school. Nabin was already in college so Mr Bijay did not have to worry about the elder son. Haksh had to leave Town High School and join a Convent School that was in his father's village. The boy was disappointed because the change in residence meant he would not be able to see Smruti anymore.

Mr Bijay had decided to shift the family to the village before the board examinations of Haksh could start but for some reason he changed the decision. He decided to shift the house after Haksh's board exams ended . He did not want Haksh's studies to be hampered. Mr. Bijay tried to bring Haksh back to Town High School but that was not possible.

Chapter 14
Bumped into

* * *

MARCH,2009
A SCHOOL IN PADAMPUR

Haksh had filled the form of the **Class Ten** board exam as a student of the Convent **School,** so he had to stay in the village . The day of the board exams came. For the board examination, the Government Girls' High School in Padampur had been allotted as the centre of the exam for the students of the Convent School in which Haksh was studying. He went to the Government Girls' High school to take the board exams. When he reached the school, he went to the notice board to see in which room he had to take the exam. He found his roll number was among the students who were taking the examination in a hall in the school. Haksh went to the hall and searched for his place. He saw his roll number was written on a desk. He sat in the chair placed near the desk. The question papers and **the** answer sheets were distributed according to the scheduled time. Haksh began to answer the questions when the writing time started . After the exam was over, Haksh walked out of the exam hall. While walking out, he saw Smruti pass in front of him. He was left with his eyes wide open at the sight of Smruti. He **saw** her after a very long time. Haksh returned home with a bright smile on his face.

He saw the exam timetable stuck to the wall in his room in order to see **when the next exam was** . The next exam was after two days. After two days, Haksh went to the Government Girls' High School very early and waited for Smruti's arrival.

After reaching the school, he parked his bike in the parking lot and looked at the entrance gate. When Smruti entered the school, Haksh looked at her. After Smruti entered the school building, Haksh entered the building. On all the exam days he would **enter** the school building after Smruti entered the building. It seemed as if Smruti was his lady luck.

On the day of the English paper, Haksh was very tensed. He wanted to do well in the English paper as it was his favourite subject. After handing over the examination answer sheet to the exam supervisor, Haksh was walking out of the exam hall reading the questions in the question paper and **trying to recall** what answers he had written in the answer sheet.

Bump!

Haksh was so engrossed in reading the questions and recalling what answers he had written that he bumped against someone. He raised his eyes from the question paper and was left shocked. In front of him was Smruti. He had bumped into Smruti. Smruti looked at Haksh with eyes wide open . Both of them kept looking at each other for some seconds before regaining their composure and walking away. Haksh was unable to believe he had bumped into Smruti. He pinched himself several times to ensure he was not dreaming.

"I hit Smruti **!** " said Haksh to himself, in disbelief. "Oh dear , I hit Smruti!"

It took him some time to realise that he had really hit Smruti. He forgot all his worries of the exam and went home smiling.

It was the last day of the board exams of class ten. Haksh reached the Government Girls' High School. He entered the examination hall after seeing Smruti. That was the last day of the board exams; Haksh was feeling a bit light in his mind. He answered the questions and came out of the exam hall after the writing time was over. That day ,too, Smruti passed in front of him. Smruti had been taking her board exams in the hall that was adjacent to the one in which Haksh was taking his exam. Haksh was happy to see Smruti. As the exams were over, Haksh decided to see her as long as he could. He walked out of the school building and stood at a place from where he could see Smruti without **letting** her notice him. She was with her friends. She walked upto the entrance gate of the school. There was a crowd at the entrance gate as parents had come to take their children home.

"I don't know whether I will be able to see you anymore or not ;but you will always be in my heart. Smruti, I will never forget you", said Haksh to himself ,looking at the girl.

Smruti's friends left her alone as their respective parents came to take them. Smruti was standing near the entrance gate waiting for someone to take her home. Haksh was thinking of riding his bike and stopping in front of her in order to offer her a lift, but the boy decided to control his emotions and not to do anything stupid in front of Smruti.

There were three boys who were standing near the entrance gate. They were not school boys. The trio were passing comments on girls. Haksh saw one of **them** say something to Smruti. The smile on Smruti's face turned sour. Haksh knew Smruti had been eve-teased. A car came. Smruti's father was driving it. He opened the door. Smruti got into the car and left. Haksh looked at the eve-teasers.

Once the school children left the school,the eve – teasers left the entrance gate. Haksh was the last person to leave the school premises.

The three boys were walking casually. They went to a roadside shop and sat on a bench. Haksh was watching their movement. He halted his bike and looked at the three boys. He saw them sipping tea from the roadside shop. Haksh looked at the garbage that had been dumped nearby. There were four rejected CFL bars. He got down from the bike and collected them.

MARCH, 2009
A TEA SHOP IN PADAMPUR

The three eve teasers were sitting on the bench and sipping tea while **talking**. Haksh came from behind and smashed a CFL bar on the head of one of the three boys . **The** other two boys could not understand anything. Haksh did not let them realise what just happened. He brought down the second CFL bar on the head of the second boy. The boy gave out a loud cry of pain. The third boy was about to get up from the bench in order to escape, but Haksh did not let him do so. He smashed the third CFL bar on that boy's head. The third boy was the one who had passed a comment on Smruti, so Haksh smashed the fourth CFL on that boy's head. The three boys shouted in pain. They used foul language on Haksh, and even he dipped his hands in dirt and abused in retaliation.

A crowd gathered in that area. Haksh was at an advantage. In that area all knew Nabin, Haksh's elder brother. So, Haksh was not a stranger to the people. The friends of the three eve-teasing boys came to attack Haksh, but Haksh too had supporters among the crowd. A fight broke out. In the fight Haksh was hit by a wooden plank on his right leg. The fight ended with all the eve teasers being beaten black and blue. Haksh was lying on the ground injured. He was helped by some people to stand up from the ground. His right leg was giving a lot of pain. Haksh had to be taken to **hospital**, where it was declared his right leg had been fractured. Nabin brought Haksh home.

"What was the use to fight?" asked Mrs Namita while

serving food to Haksh.

The boy said he could not tolerate the language the three boys were using on a girl. Haksh was free from the botheration of reading books for a couple of months.

MAY,2009
A NET CAFE

Haksh and Mr Bijay went to an internet cafe in the afternoon to check the results. Haksh was not feeling tensed as he knew he had performed well in the examination. Mr Bijay parked his bike in front of a net cafe.

" I have to use a computer ," said Haksh to the boy at the counter . The latter pointed his finger at the computer that was free for use. Haksh operated the computer to get his mark sheet. While checking his marks, a queer thought occurred to his mind.

"Let me check Smruti's score?" thought Haksh.

Haksh could check the marks of Smruti without any difficulty. Both of them were students of the State Board of Education. Haksh told Chinmay, who was Smruti's classmate, to get **Smruti's** exam roll number. Haksh got his marks from the website of the State Board of Education. He entered Smruti's roll number and got her marks too. He calculated Smruti's percentage of marks. The girl had got something between eighty and ninety percent. Haksh calculated his own percentage. He had got seventy-six percent in the board examination.

There was another boy in the cafe. He was working as the assistant to **the** boy who was at the counter. Haksh told the assistant to get a print out of the mark sheet. The boy got the print out. After getting the print copy of the mark sheet, Haksh left the computer he was operating. As he stood up from the stool infront of the computer, **he** caught sight of Smruti and her father. Smruti saw Haksh and turned her face away.

She had come to the cafe to get her mark sheet. Her father told the boy at the counter to get Smruit's mark sheet. The boy told his assistant to get the work done. The assistant did not take much time in getting the mark sheet for Smruti. Smruti's father was engrossed in looking at her mark sheet while Smruti was looking at Haksh and vice-versa. Mr Bijay was waiting for Haksh outside the cafe. Haksh smiled at Smruti, but the latter was scowling at him. She turned her face towards her father in order to avoid eye contact with Haksh. Haksh paid the boy at the counter and left the cafe.

"How have you performed in the exam?" asked Mr Bijay.

Haksh handed over the mark sheet to his father. Mr Bijay looked at the marks, **and** then looked at Haksh.

"Your performance is **all right** . Try to improve in the plus two stage of your studies" said Mr Bijay to Haksh.

"Yes, Papa ," said Haksh.

Bijay was not like other parents who'd bash up the kids over marks.

MAY, 2009
PADAMPUR

After the results of the board exams were out, Haksh applied for Science in the plus two stage of his education. He filled the admission form of Anchal College. The notification about his admission would be out after two months. In these two months Haksh did not touch any book. He wanted to play, but in a different way. Till that time he was happy in going to the field that was near the house or just going on an outing with his friends, but now he wanted to play the game of cricket in the big playground in the town.

He asked his friends for suggestions. All the boys agreed to play cricket in a big playground. It had houses near its boundary wall. Madhurja, a relative of Haksh, was living in one of the buildings located near the big playground. He invited Haksh to play in the field. Haksh and his friends befriended the other boys who came to the field to play cricket. Haksh would go to the playground every afternoon from two to five and play the game of cricket.

MAY ,2009
NEAR A PLAYGROUND

One afternoon, Haksh was cycling towards the playground. He was humming a song. While passing in front of a building, he wanted to buy a chocolate. Parking the cycle near a shop he got down from it. He bought the chocolate and returned to his cycle. The boy was about to sit on the bicycle seat when he caught sight of Smruti on the other side of the road. She was standing in front of the gate of a building. Haksh's eyes and mouth became wide open out of surprise.

Smruti was standing outside the gate of the building. She had a container in her hand. A beggar woman was standing infront of her. The beggar woman had a bag in her hand. Smruti poured the rice into the bag before entering the building. Haksh kept looking at the building.

"So, she lives here" said Haksh. He was overjoyed at the sight of her. He could not play properly in that day's match as his mind was lost in the world of imagination. This cost his team the match.

Haksh did not mind the defeat in the cricket match as his mind was somewhere else. The boy wanted to see Smruti everyday near that building. His wish was granted. Haksh went to the playground every day. He would see the girl standing on the roof of the building in which she lived . **Sometimes** he would see her standing outside the gate and talking with her friends and sometimes he would see her having an evening walk with her mother. Every time Haksh looked at the girl, he smiled. Smruti saw him but never smiled back.

As Haksh saw Smruti everyday in the afternoon, he thought he would be getting a chance to see her as long as he kept going to the playground, but he was wrong. A time came when he could not spot Smruti for days together. This saddened Haksh. The boy would halt his bicycle near the building and wait for some fifteen to twenty minutes with the hope of getting a glimpse of the girl, but the girl would not come out of the building. The girl was not seen taking any evening walk or standing on the roof. A few weeks passed, Haksh was unable to see Smruti. He thought the girl might have gone to some distant place with her family for an outing. One month was about to pass and Haksh was still not able to spot Smruti anywhere near the building. This left him wondering what could have happened to the girl.

"What happened, brother? You are not playing properly these days **?** " asked Madhurja to Haksh one evening.

Both the boys were returning from the play ground after a game of cricket.

"Does any girl named Smruti live in this locality near the playground?" asked Haksh to Madhurja.

"Which Smruti?" asked Madhurja. "There are a number of girls with the name Smruti in this locality"

"The one who used to study in Saraswati Sishu Vidyamandir. The school that falls on the way **to** Barikel , " said Haksh.

"Now, I **got the girl you** are referring to. She lives in our neighbourhood , " said Madhurja. "But why are you asking about her?"

"She was a friend of mine , " Haksh lied. "I used to see her while on my way to the playground , but now she is not visible anymore"

"Smruti and her family have left the town. They have gone to Patnagarh **.**"

"How did you know that?"

"Smruti's cousin brother is my friend"

"When will they return?"

"I have no idea. They may not return as they have left the place in order to get Smruti admitted in some good college for her plus two education."

Haksh heaved a **long** sigh after hearing this.

Chapter 15
Anchal college

* * *

JUNE, 2009
PLACE: PADAMPUR

After knowing that he would not be able to see Smruti anymore Haksh was not interested in anything. He would come to the playground and keep looking at the building ,where he used to see Smruti.

Several days after, Haksh had to go to a college for his plus two level of education. It was the Anchal College. He woke up early in the morning after listening to the alarm bell of his clock.

"Today you have to go to the college and confirm that your name is in the list of those who got admission" said Mr Bijay.

"Papa, you got the intimation letter, then why this joke?" asked Haksh.

"I have got the intimation, but it is always good to check. Errors do take place. You might not have got a place in any college and you might have got the intimation by mistake" said Mr Bijay.

Nabin laughed at Haksh, when he heard this from Mr. Bijay.

"The amount of nuisance Haksh does always keep me expecting for some kind of trouble or other" said Nabin.

Haksh wore a t-shirt and jeans. Before leaving, he sat on his bed and pulled out his old school bag. He opened the bag. It had a number of love letters and a number of chocolate wrappers in it. These were given to him by his friends who tried to help him in his love affair with Smruti. He was supposed to give them to Smruti, but he kept them instead. He read the contents of some of the letters before putting them into the bag. He pulled out a diary. He turned the last page of the diary. This diary was used to write the notes dictated in the coaching classes. He looked the last page of the diary. On that page "Smruti" had been written in beautiful handwriting.

"I don't know whether you felt my love or not, but be sure I will love you always even if you don't love me" said Haksh looking at Smruti's name. He planted a kiss on the name before closing the diary and putting it in his bag. He kissed the school bag and said "I love you Smruti". He pushed the bag under his bed and left the room.

Haksh would study in the Anchal College,a famous science college in Padampur , for two years in order to complete his plus two.

It could never be confirmed if Smruti ever nurtured any feelings for Haksh even if the boy did all sorts of nuisance to get her attention, but there was no doubt about Haksh being in love with her. He was in love with the girl even if he had not seen her for several days. The way in which he had kept the letters and the chocolate wrappers it seemed he was determined to keep Smruti's memories alive in his mind. Perhaps, that was the way he wanted to prove his love for her.

Chapter 16
Bus stop

* * *

AUGUST, 2011
PADAMPUR

It was dark. The grass was wet. The road was damp. A small stream of water was flowing on the road. It flowed from some damaged water pipe. The damage was due to the rain that took place the previous night. The rain had brought an end to the scorching heat of the summer.

When it rains, a cold breeze begins to blow. The cold breeze is always soothing and it has the ability to make people fall asleep. Haksh was sleeping in his room. The alarm bell rang. The boy stopped the alarm and went back to sleep.

"Wake up you lazy one!" shouted Nabin. "We have to catch the bus!"

Haksh woke up and left his room.

At five in the morning, Haksh was sitting in the kitchen having his breakfast.

"Do not be involved in any kind of nuisance" said Mrs Namita while serving food to Haksh.

"I will not be involved in any nuisance outside" said Haksh.

"As if you are going to keep your words" said Nabin, teasing.

"Nabin, don't make fun of Haksh. He is going away

for some months. Let him eat comfortably. He will get to eat from his mother's hand after a very long time" said Mrs .Namita.

Before leaving home, Haksh touched the feet of Mr Bijay and Mrs Namita. The parents blessed their younger son. Nabin was waiting on the TVS bike. Haksh sat as the pillion rider and waved his hand to his parents as Nabin started the bike. The brothers left.

AUGUST , 2011

A BUS STOP IN PADAMPUR

Both the brothers got down at the bus stop and were waiting for the arrival of the bus.

"Read your lessons and get good marks" said Nabin.

"Yes, brother" said Haksh.

"If the graduation is over with good marks, then rest of your life will pass comfortably"

"I know"

"You know everything even then you invite trouble"

Haksh did not say anthing.

"Don't get involved in fights and quarrels. Be a simple boy" said Nabin.

He kept advising Haksh.

"Why isn't the bus coming? I am getting tired of all this advice" thought Haksh.

A loud horn was audible. It was the bus's horn. Haksh's eyes lit up with joy. Nabin stopped speaking to Haksh and looked at the bus. The bus would go from Padampur to Sambalpur. It halted at the bus stop. The passengers got into it. Haksh also got into the bus.

"Ring me after reaching Sambalpur" said Nabin.

"Okay brother " said Haksh while entering the bus.

AUGUST, 2011

SAMBALPUR

The bus left Padampur. It was afternoon by the time

the bus reached the government bus stand of Sambalpur. Haksh got down from the bus and stretched his hands to get rid of his exhaustion.

Chapter 17
The dorm

* * *

AUGUST,2011
SAMBALPUR

Haksh hired an auto rickshaw and came to the area called Phatak, the place where railway tracks run under an over bridge. A college was located near the over bridge. The name of the college was G. M (autonomous)College. Haksh got down from the auto rickshaw and paid the driver. He headed to one of the shops that had opened under the over bridge. It was a small shop that sold tobacco, gutkha, cigarettes and pan masala. Haksh purchased four packets of pan masala and left the shop. His next stoppage was a hotel that had opened below the over bridge. He entered the hotel and ordered for lunch.

"Bring lunch" said the owner to one of the boys working in the hotel.

The boy brought a bowl of rice, two small utensils having curry and dal in it. Haksh ate the food. He paid the owner of the hotel and left. He went to a lane that ran deep into the locality called Gopalmal. The boy halted infront of a three storey building. The name of the building was "Hridayam Boys' Dorm". Haksh's father had booked a room for him in this dorm. He opened the gate and went to the room where he had to live. There were two boys in the room who were from G. M College.

"Namaste, bro" said Haksh entering the room. The other two boys greeted him. Haksh put his luggage on the wooden bed. There were three large beds in the room.

"When did you join this dorm?" asked Mahesh, a boy who was Haksh's roommate. Mahesh knew Haksh as both were from Padampur.

"My father had arranged it a month ago after it was confirmed that I would be doing my graduation in G. M College" said Haksh.

"In which department are you going to do your graduation?" asked Mahesh.

"In the Department of English" said Haksh.

Haksh changed his clothes and went to the bathroom wearing a towel. The dorm was of three storeys. The name of its owner was Mr Vikram Mishra. He lived with his family in the ground floor. The boys who had come from outside lived in the upper two storeys. The dorm had another extension which was a few metres away from Hirdayam Boys' Dorm. The name of that dorm was "Hari Om Boys' Dorm". This was a four storyed dorm that had been newly built.

Haksh had his bath and returned to his room. He opened his travel bag and took out his clothes from it. He wore some casuals and relaxed on the bed.

AUGUST 2011
THE COLLEGE PLAYGROUND

In the evening, Haksh came out of the dorm to have a walk. He wanted to see the city of Sambalpur and meet some new people. He entered the campus of G.M College. There was a vast playground with grass on it. People were walking on the grass. There were some boys who were playing cricket on the field. Students were coming out of the college. Haksh stood at one place and kept looking at the students. The boys were in blue shirts and black trousers and the girls were in a coffee coloured kameez and white salwar. They had white dupattas covering their shoulders. While looking at two girls who were walking out of the college Haksh felt one of them resembled Smruti.

The world is a strange place. We have several cases when we come across people who are the lookalikes of others. In history we have come across a number of instances where many people have kept lookalikes with them for safety.

When Haksh saw Smruti's lookalike he was taken aback. "What is she doing here?" thought Haksh, surprised. Initially he thought the girl was Smruti, but it took him some time to realise the girl was not Smruti. The girl was too slim.

"This girl looks so slim. Smruti is not that slim" said Haksh to himself when he realised he was looking at someone else.

In the market we have a term called Made in China. This is a popular term because the Chinese have the skill of making duplicates of anything original. Haksh kept looking at Smruti's lookalike. "She might not be Smruti, but atleast she looks like Smruti. She is in G. M College. I will definitely find out **her details** " said Haksh to himself. He began to follow the girl on foot. He kept a long distance between the girl and himself, so that the girl does not notice him.

"What should I call her **?**" thought Haksh. "I think Chinese Smruti would be the perfect name for her" he added.

The girl walked towards the over bridge. She crossed the railway tracks and entered a shop. Haksh crossed the railway tracks and halted near the shop. He saw the girl purchase something. He walked some steps away from the shop and waited for the girl to come out. The girl came out of the shop and walked in front of Haksh. She turned towards a lane to the left and entered a building. Haksh entered the lane and stood in front of that building . It was written "SHINE LADIES' DORM" in big bold letters on the building.

"So this Chinese Smruti lives in a ladies dorm" said

Haksh.

"Hey you!" shouted the watchman of the dorm. He walked upto him with a baton in his hand. Haksh stood still.

"What are you looking at?" asked the watchman.

"Brother, whom to contact in order to get a place here. I have a sister who is searching for a place to live in Sambalpur" said Haksh.

"What is she doing?" asked the watchman.

"M. Phil in English" said Haksh.

"Bring the girl and meet the owner of the building" said the watchman.

"Okay" said Haksh and left the place. His lie worked. He thanked his luck for escaping the watchman's beating.

AUGUST ,2011
SAMBALPUR

Haksh returned to the Hridayam Boys' dorm. His roommates saw him smiling and asked what **the reason behind it was**.

"There is no reason behind it" said Haksh. "Today I met people who would be studying graduation with me for the next three years, so I am happy"

Haksh lay on the bed. He was unable to sleep as his mind was thinking about Smruti's lookalike.

The next day, Haksh decided to go to G. M college .The teachers had started teaching the students some weeks back. Haksh was late in coming to Sambalpur in order to join the classes, but there was nothing to worry as the teachers had not done much progress in the classroom. The main reason behind this was the shortage in the teaching staff. A number of people from the teaching staff of the department had retired and the remaining few were in charge of tasks other than just teaching.

After having bath, Haksh rubbed himself dry. He took out his uniform from the travel bag and wore it.

"Remember to take your identity card with you" said Mahesh.

"What for?" asked Haksh.

"Suppose you are asked for it for some reason, then you will have to show the card. A lot of incidents take place in the college which do not concern studies. There are instances of outsiders entering the campus and harassing girls and boys. Suppose anything of that sort takes place and the police takes action then you will be in trouble"

"Okay, okay" said Haksh. He took out his identity card from his travel bag and put it in his shirt pocket.

He left the dorm, crossed the railway tracks and crossed the entrance gate of the college. Other students were entering the college building.

"Going to class is not my only objective, it's one of my objectives. My main objective is that girl" said Haksh to himself while walking on the corridors of the college building.

He stood near an iron grill and saw the writing **"Department of English"** on the top of a door that was some feet away from the iron grill.

"So, this is the English Department" said Haksh and headed towards the classroom.

While walking he saw there were several other classrooms on the way to the Department of English. These classrooms belonged to the **Department of Sanskrit** . Haksh entered the Department of English. The entrance of the department was having iron grills. The department had five rooms. There were four on the left and one on the right. Out of the four on the left, three were classrooms and one was a staff room. The room on the right was a big hall, where seminars were held. The doors of the classrooms were closed.

Haksh went close to the doors and began to listen what was going on inside the class rooms. He heard the voice of the teachers.

"I am late. Tomorrow, I will be early in coming to the class" said Haksh to himself and left the department.

Chapter 18
Forgot everything

* * *

AUGUST, 2011
INSIDE GANGADHAR MEHER AUTONOMOUS COLLEGE

Haksh kept wandering in the building in order to see the various departments in the building. The college building had a number of classrooms in the two-storey building. There were several classrooms, four halls and two large galleries in the college building.

"This is such a big college" said Haksh.

The college building had two main entrances . One entrance was the one on which "Gangadhar Meher (Autonomous) college" had been written. This entrance gate was almost in front of the T.F BOYS' **HOSTEL**. The other entrance to the building was near the Girls' common room. While walking near the girls' common room, Haksh saw a number of students walking out of the college building. These were the students who were coming out of their classrooms. Haksh stood at one place with the hope of seeing the lookalike of Smruti. He saw the girl. The girl was walking with her friends. Once Haksh caught sight of her, he forgot everything and began to follow her from a distance. The girl walked out of the **main** entrance gate of the college which was close to the railway tracks that went under the over bridge.

AUGUST,2011
PHATAK

One could enter the college premises from two sides. One **main entrance gate** was near the starting end of the over bridge and the other **main entrance gate** was near a small Hanuman Temple that was close to the railway tracks that ran a few meters away from the boundary wall of the college. She left the college from the gate that was close to the railway tracks. Haksh followed her. A number of shops had opened under the over bridge. The girls entered a shop that sold fast food. Haksh stood outside the shop for some time. The girls remained inside the shop. Haksh entered the shop. The shopkeeper was selling cakes, patties and noodles. There were other food items as well.

"Brother what is the cost of the patties?" asked Haksh.

"Veg patties or non-veg patties" asked the shop keeper.

"Veg Patties" said Haksh.

"Eleven"

"Non -veg"

"Fifteen"

"Give me the veg one"

While the shopkeeper was busy in taking out the veg patties from the oven, Haksh glanced at **Smruti's** lookalike while pretending to be looking at the other things available in the shop. The lookalike was talking a lot with the other girls. The girls were talking about what all happened in the class that day. The shopkeeper gave the patties to Haksh. There was no chair to sit as the girls had occupied all of **them**. Haksh kept standing while eating his patties. The girls finished eating and left the place. Haksh, who was eating his patties slowly, finished it in a hurry. He paid the shopkeeper and left. The girls took leave of each other and dispersed. Smruti's lookalike walked towards her living place. Haksh walked towards her taking fast steps.

"Hello, you there" said Haksh coming closer to the girl.

The girl halted and looked at Haksh. She gave a puzzled look at the boy.

"You are Neeraj's sister, aren't you ? Nice to meet you. Give Neeraj brother my best wishes" said Haksh.

"Who is this Neeraj?" asked the girl.

"Neeraj....... He lives in our neighbourhood. Are you not Smruti, his sister?"

"Whom are you talking about? I don't know this Neeraj . I am not Smruti"

"Then who are you?"

"Neha"

"Sorry" said Haksh. "I thought you to be someone else."

The girl did not say anything. She walked away.

Chapter 19
Some help

* * *

AUGUST, 2011
NEAR GANGADHAR MEHER COLLEGE

Haksh kept looking at the girl go.

"So her name is Neha" said Haksh to himself.

The girl entered the lane that led to her dorm. Haksh went to his dorm. He entered his room.

"What was taught today?" asked Mahesh.

"I don't have books. How will I study?" said Haksh.

"Today in the evening go to the boys' hostel and make a few friends. They will help you in getting the books for the syllabus"

"How will I know the people of my class?"

"Just go to any of the **boys'** hostels and ask if there are any boys who are studying English Honours"

"Okay"

AUGUST,2011
ON THE PREMISES OF GANGADHAR MEHER COLLEGE

Haksh went to G. M College. He looked at the playground. A number of boys were playing there. He saw one of the boys. He felt as if he knew one of the boys who were playing cricket. The boy was holding the bat.

"Sagar bro!" shouted Haksh.

The boy who was holding the bat looked at Haksh and gave a bright smile.

"Arey Haksh! You?" said Sagar.

Haksh was heading towards Sagar, when the latter told Haksh to wait for a minute. Haksh halted on his steps. The bowler bowled the ball. Sagar did not try to hit the ball. He moved aside and the ball hit the wickets. Sagar was out. He gave the bat to the next boy who was to bat and headed towards Haksh.

"Why did you do that?" asked the boy, who was the wicket keeper.

"I have to meet that boy from our village" said Sagar while walking towards Haksh. He came near Haksh with a wide smile.

"Haksh, how are you?" asked Sagar patting the back of Haksh.

"Brother, you got yourself out to meet me"

"That's a not a big problem. We had some one or two overs left"

"What were you playing?"

"Test cricket"

"Have you been batting all the day long?"

"No"

"Then?"

"We play it in our way. We play in the afternoons"

"Strange. You have your own rules to play the game of test cricket"

"So when did you come here?"

"Yesterday"

"What are you doing here?"

"I am a student of the Department of English. Has my brother not told you about it?"

"No"

"Oh! He might not have felt the need of it" said

Haksh. "I need your help"

"Tell me. I am a senior student of your department"

"What?"

"Yes, I am in your department. I am doing M.A in English"

"This is great news for me"

"You can get any kind help that you want."

"I want to meet some boys who have newly joined the Department of English"

"So you are searching for first year English Honours boys ?"

"Yes"

"That's not a problem"

Sagar took Haksh to a boys' hostel that had the writing Trust Fund Boys' Hostel on its entrance gate.

He took Haksh to a room where he introduced Haksh to a boy named Naba. Naba was a second year English Honours student . Naba introduced Haksh to a boy named Gopal who was a first year English Honours student.

"Gopal, where are you from?"asked Haksh.

" From Sohela" said Gopal.

"I have missed a lot of classes. Can you help me?"

"I can take you to a boy who can help you"

"That would be grateful of you" said Haksh.

That night Haksh was happy over the fact that he would be getting some help in preparing his lessons.

Chapter 20
The meeting

* * *

AUGUST, 2011
SAMBALPUR

The next day, Haksh left his dorm early and reached college. He met Gopal in the college. Haksh attended all the classes. After the classes were over, Gopal led Haksh to a place where cycles were kept in the college. They were kept under a big tree that stood in front of the examination section of G. M College. A water reservoir stood near the tree.

"Hi Madan" said Gopal to a boy who was standing under the tree. The boy was leaning against a bicycle.

"Hi Gopal" said Madan and shook hands with Gopal.

"This is Haksh" said Gopal introducing Haksh to Madan.

"I am Madan" said Madan. He shook hands with Haksh.

"So, this is the guy who can help me" said Haksh to Gopal, referring to Madan.

"Madan is the right guy to approach. He helps others a lot" said Gopal.

"Madan, I am in deep trouble" said Haksh.

"What's your problem?" aksed Madan.

"I have missed a number of classes. I don't know how to catch up" said Haksh.

"Where were you all this time?"

"I was at home"

"Now, you are suffering because of staying at home."

"Just tell me how to deal with the situation"

"It's a long way. You will have to do a task"

"Tell me what is to be done"

"Not now. I will tell you a place where I can tell you everything"

"Which is that place?"

Madan looked at Gopal and asked "Where are Hemant and Gaurav ?"

"They are coming" said Gopal.

The boys waited for sometime before two more boys entered the cycle stand.

"Haksh" said Madan. "These two boys are Hemant and Gaurav"added Madan introducing the two boys to Haksh. Hemant and Gaurav shook hands with Haksh.

"You don't look to be belonging to this place" said Haksh, looking at Gaurav's face.

"He is from Assam" said Madan.

"Really?" said Haksh

"Yes, I am from Assam" said Gaurav.

"What made you come to Odisha?"

"My father is in the Army. His posting keeps changing from place to place, so I have to move from one educational institution to another"

"I see"

"I am Hemant" said the boy standing with Gaurav.

Haksh and Hemant shook hands. Hemant was a local boy.

"Haksh, I will help you. You have to come to join us at Hemant's house" said Madan.

"Is there any special occasion?"

"Hemant has invited us for a feast "

"Does he live there alone?"

" No"

"Then?"

"His family members have gone away to attend his aunt's marriage ceremony. He decided to stay in the house as the internal assessment exam is near" said Madan.

"I see" asked Haksh.

"Yes" said Madan.

"Then I have no problem. **We all will talk a lot and come to know about each other at Hemant's home**" said Haksh.

"You should know about Gaurav"said Madan

"What for?" asked Haksh looking at Gaurav.

"This fellow comes to college but always gets himself engaged in doing something or other with some girl in the college"said Madan.

Gaurav smiled.

"The girls over here have no brains. They just think of fair skin" said Hemant. He looked upset.

"Don't feel bad, Hemant" said Madan and patted Hemant's back.

It was decided that the boys would meet at Hemant's house. Haksh was happy that he would be able to discuss his lessons, but the joy was short lived when the meeting was cancelled because Hemant had to accompany his parents **to his aunt's** marriage ceremony. The disappointment was not permanent because Gopal informed Haksh that there will be a meeting at Hemant's house in the month of **November when his parents would be away to join the rest of their family members on a pilgrimage**.

"You may have to deal with the internal assessment on your own, but you will certainly get help for the semester exams " said Gopal to Haksh.

Haksh waited for November to come.

....

OCTOBER, 2011
SAMBALPUR

Disha entered the college and parked her bicycle under a tree. She entered the college building and sat in a hall. She looked at the ceiling of the hall for sometime then to the time by her wrist watch. The clock stuck 9:30 A.M.

The girl heaved a sigh and left the hall with her backpack. She was definitely waiting for someone, but was disappointed with the delay. She went to her department that was upstairs in the first floor. Her friends were waiting outside the department.

"Hi Disha" said Shraddha greeting the girl.

"Hi Shraddha" said Disha. The two friends entered the classroom.

The classes went on upto one p.m in the afternoon. Disha left the classroom after the classes were over.

Gaurav was standing near Hall Number One. Disha came down the steps and found Gaurav. Both of them entered Hall Number One and sat beside each other.

"Why did you delay so much?" asked Disha.

"The classes were not over" said Gaurav.

Both of them sat there looking at each other for some time. Gaurav stood up from the bench and walked out of the hall. He checked the corridor. There was no one there. There was another hall close Hall Number One. It was Hall Number Two. Gaurav walked up to Disha and held her hand.

"Come with me" said Gaurav. Disha stood up. Both of them entered **Hall Number Two** and stood near a bench holding each other in a tight embrace.

Gaurav planted a kiss on Disha's lips. He made her remove her backpack. Gaurav held her tightly close to him. Disha had a coy smile on her face. Gaurav walked out of the hall to check if there was anyone nearby. There was no one. He came back to Disha, who was standing near the black board. She opened the rubber band from her hair. Gaurav held her and pulled her closer towards the blackboard. Both of them embraced each other. Gaurav pushed Disha against the blackboard and both of them got engrossed in a lip lock

....

NOVEMBER, 2011
SAMBALPUR

"You must be able to guess what might have taken place after that" said Gaurav

"Yes, yes, I can guess it" said Hemant.

"You got involved in playing your game of love with Disha" said Haksh.

"Lust would be the appropriate word for it. Gaurav played the game of lust with that girl" said Madan eating a morsel of biryani.

The four friends were having a feast at Hemant's house. His parents had gone far away to join the rest of his family members on a pilgrimage. They were not going to return soon. Hemant was staying at home in order to prepare for the first semester which was in the month of December.

The boys were eating biryani which they had ordered from an eatery. While eating ,the boys were sharing some special moments of their lives. Gaurav, who was a womaniser, was narrating some of the relationships he had made with some girls in the college. Disha was one of those girls.

"How long did that go on?" asked Haksh. "Your game of lust with Disha"

"Two hours" said Gaurav.

"Two hours?"

"It was all about kissing and other things."

"Other things like?"

"I only used my hand on her body. You can guess"

"Now she will again try to meet you" said Madan.

"She did" said Gaurav

"How many times?"asked Hemant.

"Five" said Gaurav.

"One must admit that girl is mentally ill. Doing such things in the college in the broad day light really needs a lot of courage" said Madan.

"Yes" said Hemant.

"Disha is unable to control herself." said Haksh.

"That's the reason she does it anywhere" said Gaurav.

"Hey look at that!" said Hemant.

The four boys were watching a horror movie on the television. Maybe the movie had become intense so the boys stopped talking about Disha and focussed on watching the TV.

"I think she should get married as soon as possible" said Madan. "That will be good for her" he added referring to Disha.

"Her parents sent her to study here and you can see what she is doing" said Hemant, angrily.

"What happened, Hemant? You look upset" asked Haksh.

"He loves Disha" said Gaurav.

"Disha is unable to know the person who is in love with her but is keeping physical relationship with every other boy just for lust" said Madan.

"Hemant, you are lucky that she is not with you. Just imagine the problem you would have fallen into" said Gaurav.

"What kind of problem?"said Hemant.

"Just imagine. The girl is having relationships with a number of boys. She is cheating on them. If her parents come to know about her activities someday then think what will happen. They will punish Disha and the boys involved with her. It can be a police case." said Haksh. " You are lucky that Disha hates you. If anything wrong takes place with the girl then your name will never be mentioned." **added Haksh**

"Friend"said Madan putting his hand **on Hemant's back** . "It is never safe to keep any contact with a girl who has such dangerous relationships with others because it will prove disastrous in the long run. If she is caught doing such dirty things, she will get married. She has nothing to bother about, but you have to face a lot of things. A police case can hamper your employment. Just think about it" he added.

Hemant did not say anything. He ate his food silently. After eating the food, Gaurav entered a room to have a talk with Sandhya over the phone. Sandhya was the only girl whom Gaurav loved a lot. Haksh went to the bed room and slept. Madan was a diehard gamer. He played computer games in Hemant's computer. Hemant kept watching movie after movie till his eyes began to ache and he fell asleep in the TV room. The next day the boys woke up at nine in the morning. Haksh was sent to bring food. He rode Hemant's bicycle and went to bring food from the hotels that were made near G. M College. After sunset Haksh was again sent to the area near G. M college to bring food.

Haksh reached Phatak on the bicycle. He halted in front of a shop and looked at the time by his wrist watch. It was six in the evening. The boy parked his bicycle near the shop and entered a hotel.

He ordered for rice, curry and chicken.

"Brother pack the food" said Haksh to hotel's owner. The boy was standing near the hotel counter when he caught sight of Neha. The girl passed in front of the hotel.

"Brother how long will it take to arrange the food?" asked Haksh to the owner. He was getting impatient to follow Neha.

The waiter brought the food. Haksh took the food and left the hotel after paying the owner. He put the food in Hemant's backpack. Neha had not gone too far. Haksh began to cycle slowly towards her from behind. Neha was walking towards the row of shops that were near an ATM machine. They all were located on one end of the over bridge. Haksh saw a boy smoking on the side of the road. The boy passed some foul comment on Neha. Haksh heard the comment and became angry. He sped up and halted infront of the boy. "Do you know who that girl is?" asked Haksh to the boy. The boy had not expected this. He gave a blank look to Haksh.

"That's your mother, you bastard. That's your mother" said Haksh, mocking the boy.

The boy became angry and came towards Haksh. Haksh got down from the cycle. The boy punched Haksh. The latter did not fight back. The boy uttered some foul language. Haksh left the place. He reached Hemant's house and gave the backpack to Hemant.

That night the boy's revelled. They ate the food and drank cold drinks. They spent the day watching movies and cricket matches. Haksh was in another room. He was busy having a chat with someone over the phone. The other day Haksh went to college. He tried to track down the boy, who had passed foul comments on Neha the previous day. He saw that boy near a shop. Once he saw the boy, he kept following the boy for some distance. The boy lived somewhere in the slum that was in front of the college. Haksh returned to college after following the boy upto some distance. He went to the P.G Boys' Hostel and entered Sagar's room.

"When are you coming?" asked Haksh.

"In the afternoon or may be **in** the evening. We know that boy" said Sagar. "His name is Tangi"

It was sunset. Haksh come out of the college. He waited for Tangi to appear. The boy always stood near the over bridge and kept passing comments at girls. He had his friends with him . Haksh came back to the P.G Hostel to inform Sagar about Tangi. Tangi was busy passing **comments** on the girls who passed in front of him. All of a sudden he found himself surrounded.

"You were saying something to girls"said Sagar.

Tangi was taken aback. Haksh walked towards him and punched the boy. A fight broke out. Haksh and his supporters fought with Tangi. Tangi was beaten black and blue. Neha was walking that way. She saw the sight of Haksh beating Tangi. The people living in the area wished someone beat Tangi. They supported the action of the college boys.

The next day Haksh came to college. He had injury marks on his hands. He saw Neha in the college. The girl was walking.

"Neha" called Haksh.

The girl halted and looked at Haksh.

"Are you being eve-teased by any boy near the over bridge anymore?" asked Haksh.

"No" said Neha.

"That's fine" said Haksh.

"But what was the need of doing all that?"asked Neha.

"I don't know. I felt bad when I heard the foul language that the boy was using on you" said Haksh.

"He may try to harm you" said Neha.

"No way. A number of people know me here" said Haksh.

"But what was the need for all this. We girls tolerate all such eve-teasing everyday" said Neha.

"Just don't know why I felt bad about it"

"Thank you for it"

"Both of us have to spend three long years in the college. If you develop the habit of thanking me then you will get tired of thanking me."

"Really?"

"Because we both are going to be in the same college for a very long time"

"In which department do you study?"

"English" said Haksh. "And you?"

"Hindi"

There was the Compulsory English Class. In that class, all the students studying Arts had to go to the halls.

Haksh entered Hall Number One. He found Neha in it. Both of them looked at each other and smiled.

"I think both of us will be meeting each other almost daily" said Haksh. Neha did not say anything. She just blushed.

After the English Honours classes were over Haksh purposefully waited for the Hindi classes to be over. After the Hindi Honours classes were over, he saw Neha walking out of the college campus. He walked with her.

"Where do you live?" asked Haksh.

"In a dorm" said Neha.

"Me too"

"In which dorm do you live?"

"Hridayam dorm"

"I live in Shine Ladies' dorm .Your dorm is very far from ours"

"Yes it is. But it helps me in doing a bit of a morning walk"said Haksh

Neha could not stop herself from laughing. "What a point of view!" exclaimed Neha.

Both of them walked together. They ate gupchup in a stall before telling good bye to each other.

Haksh enterd his room in the dorm. He took out his file of certificates from his bag. In that file was a photograph of Smruti, which Chinmay had given him. Haksh looked at Smruti's photo and said "May be the love for you has not ended in me. I might not have got you here, but I have someone who looks just like you." He kissed the photograph and added, "To accept my love or not is your choice , but to keep loving you is my determination"

It appeared as if Haksh was going to fall for anyone who looked like Smruti.

Did Neha's entry in Haksh's life mean the boy was never **going to** meet Smruti anymore in his life?

He is with Neha because she looks like Smruti. Neha

maybe looking like Smruti, but she could be something else from inside.

Will Haksh forget the real Smruti and lose himself **to** her look-alike?

Chapter 21
Tensed mind

* * *

SEPTEMBER, 2011
SAMBALPUR

The month of September came. It was the time for the first internal assessment. Haksh was worried as he had delayed a lot in arranging the books mentioned in the syllabus of the first semester. **The internal assessment was a prelude to the semester exam**. Madan had prepared some notes. He gave them to Haksh. The day the internal assessment exam was over Haksh called Madan to a shop near the **main entrance gate** of the college.

"Brother, two pieces of veg patties" said Haksh to the shop keeper.

"Okay" said the shopkeeper.

Haksh told Madan to sit in a chair. Madan sat in a chair. Haksh had invited him for a treat. Haksh sat in another chair.

"Thank you, Madan" said Haksh. "Thanks for your help. I won't be getting single digit numbers because of you."

"Oh really?" said Madan.

"I had given up all my hopes about scoring good marks" said Haksh. "Why? What was the problem? Were you not prepared for the internal assessment?"

"No" said Haksh.

"You do not even come to the classroom. I have rarely seen you in the classroom" said Madan.

The shopkeeper gave the boys a veg patties each. The two boys began to eat the food.

"When are the first semester exams going to be held ?" asked Haksh.

"I think either in the month of November or December" said Madan.

Haksh stopped eating and looked at Madan. Madan looked at the expression on Haksh's face. The expression was of surprise.

"What happened?" asked Madan.

Haksh resumed eating his patties and said he will badly need some help in his lessons as he may not be able to cover the vast syllabus of the first semester **examination**.

"Why?" asked Madan. "You have so much time"

"I need the help of a coaching centre" said Haksh. He had been habituated to the culture of going to coaching centres. Now, he was finding it difficult to prepare for the exam without the help of one. Madan assured to prepare notes for the boy. Haksh thanked Madan for that. The two friends finished eating the pieces of **patties .** Haksh began to attend the classes regularly . He had two months to prepare properly for the first semester. He went to the boys' hostel to get notes and old question papers from the senior students of his department.

One day after the classes were over,Haksh was walking out of the college building. He saw Hemant walking slowly towards the entrance gate of the college. The boy was walking with his head downcast, as if he was in some sort of intense grief. Haksh walked towards Hemant.

"Hi Hemant" said Haksh putting his hand on the shoulder of Hemant's shoulder .

"Yes, Haksh" said Hemant with a smile on his face.

"You look so sad"

"Exam is near" said Hemant.

"Is the exam bothering you or is Disha bothering you too?"

Hemant heaved a sigh and said "It's Disha"

"Try to focus on the lessons . The exam is important."

"I will try"

Haksh took Hemant to a fast food shop. The two boys ate some fast food and left. While leaving Hemant wore a smile on his face. Haksh paid for the food. Hemant left the place on his bicycle.

Haksh returned to his dorm. Haksh was too busy for his examinations. He did not have time even for Neha. He saw her every day in the Hall Number One,which was meant for Compulsory English students. Both of them would smile and greet each other. The time table for the first semester exam was put on the notice board. The exam was in December. Haksh was looking at the timetable.

Madan was standing near him.

"How are you feeling about the exam ?" asked Madan.

"Nervous" said Haksh. "For the first time I am feeling afraid of the examination."

"Be reading my notes" said Madan.

The first semester exam came. It was over in two weeks. The day the examination ended Haksh rushed to his room, packed up his luggage and left for Padampur by the afternoon bus. When his roommates asked why he was leaving in a hurry, he said he wanted to relax his tensed mind.

Smruti was not in Padampur, so there was no chance for Haksh to do anything courageous to see Smruti or to get her attention. Haksh spent the time in playing cricket. A new computer was purchased. Nabin had got a job in a mill. He was also working as a contractor , and was being paid well for it. He joined a political party as a volunteer. One knows what happens when a person joins a political party. The person begins to earn a lot of money.

Politicians always have to keep henchmen. These henchmen end up getting well paid and start their own business. Some henchman had opened a business of real estate in Padampur and Nabin decided to join the business. He got money from the henchman. Haksh did not bother about what Nabin did. He was happy in playing computer games . He played games in the computer till afternoon. When the clock struck two in the afternoon, he left his home and went to the playground. All his friends were now college students. All of them met in the playground to play cricket.

Chapter 22
Book fair

* * *

JANUARY,2012
SAMBALPUR

Haksh was back to Sambalpur in the first week of the New Year. This time he had to prepare for the second semester exam . Preparing for the second semester was not a big botheration for him as the semester was going to be held in the month of June and now it was January. So, he had a lot of time for preparation.

Haksh entered his dorm. Mahesh was already in the room.

"Didn't you go to **your** village in the holidays after the first semester?"asked Haksh.

"Yes, I went. I went home, stayed there for four days and came back" said Mahesh.

"Have the classes started in our department?"asked Haksh.

"I don't know"

"I will go to the college in the fourth week of the month."

"You are again going to miss something important by not going to classes."

"No problem. The second semester is in **June** . I have a lot of time to catch up with the lessons"

"Your wish"

Haksh had bath and slept on his bed. He woke up in the evening and left the dorm. He went to the Trust Fund Hostel. He headed to Naba's room. Naba was sitting in a chair and reading a book.

Haksh greeted him. Naba greeted Haksh.

"Brother, can you give me notes for **the** second semester **exam** ?" asked Haksh.

"Yes, of course" said Haksh.

Both the boys talked about various things. While talking, Haksh asked about the arrangement of books **for the second semester exams** .

"Wait for the book fair. It will start after two or three days. Try to find the books that are in your syllabus."

"For how many days does this fair go on ?"

"Some ten days or so. The fair goes on up to the fourth week of the month"

"Hmm...."

"And one more thing"

"Yes"

"Try to get the books of the rest semesters in advance"

"Okay, brother"

Haksh returned to his dorm. He talked a lot about trivial things with Mahesh. While talking he came to know that Mahesh had his eyes on a girl named Mamuni, who was his classmate. Haksh was excited to know that boys and girls of the college keep roaming around in the fair. In his mind he could imagine himself moving about with Neha, the lookalike of Smruti. That evening Haksh rang up his father and asked him to send him some money to spend in the book fair that was to come very soon.

The book fair started. A number of stalls opened in the open ground in front of G.M College. Haksh went to the fair and moved around with his classmates. Hemant, Madan and Gaurav were his friends. He moved about with them.

They would move from stall to stall and end up in the stall that sold fast food. The boys spent less on books and more on fast food.

One evening ,Hemant was looking very thoughtful while walking with Haksh in the book fair. Madan and Gaurav were present in the fair but they were roaming around.

"What's the matter Hemant? Why are you so thoughtful today?"asked Haksh to Hemant.

"Nothing" said Hemant.

Haksh could mark that Hemant was trying to control his emotions. He took Hemant to a stall and told him to look at the books and see if anything valuable could be found. Hemant began to look at the books in the stall. Haksh came out of the stall. He was looking at the faces of the people who had come to the fair. He caught sight of Neha. There was a wide smile on his face. He walked up to Neha, who was walking with her friends.

"Hi Neha" said Haksh.

"Hi" greeted Neha.

"Never saw you here. Are you coming to the fair today?" asked Haksh.

"Yes"

"Would you mind if I walk around the fair with you?"

"No,not at all" said Neha. "Why should I mind it?"

"Could I know the names of your friends?"

Neha introduced the two girls who were with her. They were Usharani and Abipsha. Both the girls shook hands with Haksh. They walked from stall to stall.

"Have you purchased any of the books that have been mentioned in the syllabus?" asked Neha.

"No, not yet. The best way to get the books in the syllabusis to order for them from the local book shops" said Haksh.

"Which book shop should we go to order for the books ?"

"Book Point, Shakti Pustak Bhandar and Good books"

Neha and Haksh talked about the books mentioned in their syllabus.

"Hey! Let's go to the fast food stall and eat something" **said Haksh**

"Yes. Let's go there" said Neha.

Neha and her two friends sat on the chairs near the stall.

"What will you people eat?" asked Haksh.

"Chowmein" said Neha.

Haksh ordered for four **plates** of chowmein. The owner of the fast food stall made the food items. Haksh brought the four plates . He gave three to the girls and kept one with him. The girls and Haksh got engaged in a gossip. Haksh came to know about Neha. She was the daughter of a land lord in Bargarh. Her ancestors used to be zamindars . Now, her father . **He** had a lot of land had opened small mills on them. Inspite of being from a very rich family the girl was not haughty. Haksh **liked** this aspect of Nehas'a character. Haksh began to admire her in his mind.

Haksh felt a hand on his right shoulder. He looked to his right side and found it to be Hemant. He looked at the girls and said"Thank you girls for the chat. We will be meeting in the college tomorrow in the Compulsory English class"

"Bring the xerox of the notes I told you. Bring them from that boy whom you call Madan. The teacher has given him some notes in front of the whole classroom" said Neha.

"Okay" said Haksh.

He stood up from the chair and left the place with Hemant.

" Feeling lucky to have so much time among girls" said Hemant after the boys had walked some distance from the fast food stall.

"I meet these girls in the Compulsory English class everyday" said Haksh.

"Oh really?"

"Yes"

"That's nice"

"Did you get anything useful from the books stalls?"

"I looked at the titles of the books, took some in my hand and turned the pages before putting them back to the shelves."

"You look disturbed today. What's the matter?"

"Today I saw Disha in the book fair. I decided to have a talk with her. The talk was not to be on love. I would have talked on other things ,but she just turned her back to me and walked away hurriedly"

"Oh so this is your problem."

"Yes."

"Look there" said Haksh pointing his hand in one direction.

Hemant looked in that direction and found Gopal and Disha. Both of them were walking together and talking .

"Hello friends" came a voice.

Haksh looked back and found Madan and Gaurav. Haksh showed them how Disha was walking with Gopal. Hemant walked towards the exit of the book fair. Gopal headed towards the exit with Disha.

"Let's not leave Hemant alone. He is very upset" said Haksh and headed towards the exit. Gaurav and Madan walked with Haksh.

Once they reached outside the book fair they saw Gopal looking at Disha. The girl sat on her cycle and left the place. Hemant was looking at Gopal. After the girl left, Hemant walked towards Gopal speedily. Gopal turned towards Hemant.

"You traitor!" shouted Hemant and gave a violent push to Gopal.

Haksh, Gaurav and Madan ran to the spot. After pushing Gopal, Hemant was walking towards the entrance gate of the college angrily. Haksh ran up to him and said "Hemant, what are you doing?"

"There is no love in my luck."said Hemant with tears in his eyes. Haksh held Hemant and pulled him towards Gopal.

Madan and Gaurav were with Gopal. Haksh told Hemant and Gopal to shake hands and embrace each other as friends. Hemant and Gopal shook hands and embraced each other. The boys sat on the grassy ground of the college and talked about the problem caused by Disha. It was decided that none was going to fight over the girl. All should keep away from her.

JANUARY , 2012
SAMBALPUR

After settling the issue between Gopal and Hemant, Haksh returned to his dorm. He narrated the incident to his roommates.

"Are you talking about that girl in that Geography department?" asked Mahesh.

"Yes" said Haksh.

"Shame on those boys for fighting over such a cheap girl" said Mahesh.

"Today those two fought over her."

"I can't believe it."

Haksh was shocked by the behaviour of Hemant. Hemant was a boy who never messed up with others. He remained away from trouble. Haksh was sad that a boy of such kind was behaving in a crazy way. The next day at college after the classes were over, Haksh called Hemant to the stage that was built near the hostel that was meant for the boys who were studying Post Graduation in the college.

The two boys sat on the stage.

"Speak out your pain Hemant . You cannot study your lessons with a diverted mind" said Haksh.

Hemant said Disha was a girl living in his neighbourhood. He saw her regularly while coming to college. He accompanied her while coming to the college. In the process he began to develop feelings for her. Hemant admitted that he was a failure in love. The boy had a history of being rejected by whichever girl he liked.

"Hemant, I will tell you one thing" said Haksh.

"Yes" said Hemant.

"I am the reason why Disha is so much attracted towards Gopal."

Hemant looked at Haksh with eyes wide open.

"Let me tell you how it happened" said Haksh.

Hemant considered Haksh to be a close friend. He was sad for what he heard, but he accepted it to be his fate and heard whatever Haksh was going to narrate.

NOVEMBER, 2011
SAMBALPUR

One day Haksh entered **Gopal's room** . Gopal was looking thoughtful.

"What happened? What's troubling you?" asked Haksh.

"Disha" said Gopal.

"Why?"

"I can't get my mind away from her?"

"Then go be with her"

"But if I be with her ,I may hurt Hemant."

"But why does that girl hate Hemant so much **?**"

"I do not know. Hemant is a good boy. He was the first among us to fall in love with her. Maybe it is his complexion that makes Disha hate him."

"What do such girls think themselves to be? The British used to do this black and white discrimination, but now we have girls like Disha doing it. Do such girls think they are from Britain?"

"I don't know. The girl talks with me a lot. Sometimes I wish to have her"

"Can you make me talk with Disha?"

"Yes"

Gopal made Haksh have a talk with Disha over the phone. Haksh spoke **to** Disha over the phone. He pretended to be Gopal's elder brother .

"What do you dislike about Hemant ?" asked Haksh during the conversation .

"He comes to my home every day in the evening. My aunt does not like it. He is a very possessive boy and I do not find him attractive." said Disha **about Hemant**.

"So what do you think about Gopal ?" asked Haksh.

"He is a simple boy. A well natured guy."

"Do you like him?"

"Yes"

"Even he likes you and wants to marry you."

Gopal was left with his mouth wide open on hearing this.

"But...."Gopal wanted to say something

"Let us do a mock marriage."Haksh interrupted him

The next day Gopal and Disha went to the temple on top of the Budharaja hill. Gopal put red vermillion on Disha's forehead and both of them embraced each other.

JANUARY, 2012
SAMBALPUR

Haksh ended his narration.

"You did all this in spite of knowing something was hurting me? You did all this after I gave you a place in my house in order to discuss about lessons with Madan?" demanded Hemant.

"I am sorry. I never thought you would take the

matter so seriously. But I must tell you one thing. I did it for one good reason" **said Haksh**

"What good reason ?"

"You are a studious boy. Gopal is not that studious. Initially, I told him to be away from Disha, but he was in no mood to listen. You are lucky to be away from that girl. Even Gopal did not know what the girl was. A few days after that mock marriage we found her with Gaurav. When we asked what was Gaurav doing with the girl we came to know both of them were in a relationship since September."

Hemant was upset. He shouted at Haksh. He called Haksh to be a boy who might not have loved anyone, a heartless fellow and many other hurtful comments. Hemant left the place promising that he would never talk with Haksh. Haksh was sad. He returned to his dorm.

"You might not have ever fallen in love with anyone, so you could not understand my pain. You are heartless" these words of Hemant were ringing in his ears.

Haksh entered his room in the dorm. Sleep did not come to his eyes. He spent the afternoon changing sides.

Chapter 23
His galatea

* * *

JANUARY, 2012
SAMBALPUR

Haksh went to the college. He went there to meet his friends and try to forget the thing that was paining him the previous day. That day he went to the classroom. He found Hemant was absent.

"The boy is badly hurt" said Haksh to himself.

After the classes were over he went to the book fair with Madan and Gaurav.

"What happened today? Why are you so thoughtful?" asked Madan.

"I am sad about Hemant. He is in a bad mental state" said Haksh.

"Then there is no need to give any explanation. I know the cause" said Gaurav.

"I am the one responsible for it" said Haksh. He told his friends about the way he had arranged the mock marriage between Gopal and Disha.

"That was so crazy of you" said Madan. "Now let's purchase some books. We have not purchased any quality book till now." He added.

"And text books related to our syllabus are rarely found in the book fair" said Haksh.

The boys separated and entered various stalls. That day they were serious about purchasing some books. Haksh entered a stall. It was a big book stall. While looking at the books he bumped against a girl. The girl turned back and looked at him. It was Neha.

"Hi!" greeted Haksh.

"Hello" said Neha.

"At least now looking for books won't be boring" said Haksh.

"Why?"

"I have got a friend like you to accompany me"

Neha blushed after hearing this. Haksh found Neha was looking at some books; she would take them from the shelf, look at their attractive covers, turn their pages then put them back on the shelves. Neha spent one hour looking at the books in that particular stall. Haksh kept walking with her without uttering anything.

"Why are you not purchasing anything?" she asked to Haksh.

"I have nothing to purchase. For me my own syllabus is too heavy to manage, so I cannot give time for other books" said Haksh. "I am here to eat something with you at the fast food stall"

"One thing about it"

"Yes, say"

"I liked the food stall ."

"Then today I will give something better"

Both of them came out from the book stall. Neha kept walking. She stopped for a while and looked around to find Haksh was missing. She looked at the book stall from which she had come out .Haksh was at the counter of the book stall. He was paying the man at the counter. After making the payment, Haksh walked towards Neha with a bag in his hand.

"What's there in the bag?" asked Neha

"Books" said Haksh.

"What books did you buy?"

"See them " said Haksh and handed over the bag to the girl. She took out the books from the bag. She was surprised to find the bag contained all the books that she had picked up from the shelves of the book stall. She had picked the books, turned their pages and returned them to the book shelves.

"Is it some kind of a surprise for me? I had picked up all these books from the bookshelf, but could not buy them as I did not have enough money"said Neha.

"Yes, it's a surprise for you" said Haksh. "They belong to you"

The girl was delighted. She thanked Haksh. Neha carried the bag with her. Haksh and Neha walked out of the book fair.

"Where are your friends?" asked Haksh.

"Today they did not come for some reason I do not know" said Neha.

"Last time you liked the fast food. Today you go to your dorm. I will give you another treat of tasty fast food" said Haksh.

"Really!" said Neha.

"Yes"

"Okay. So, I am going to my dorm. You bring the food"

"I will need your number to ring you when I bring the food"

"Okay"

Haksh got her phone number. Neha went to her dorm. Haksh went to"TOP N TOWN", a cafe that had opened near Hotel Saket. He ordered for two pizzas. It took half an hour for the two pizzas to be

made. He got them parcelled and reached Phatak. He informed Neha **about** his arrival over the phone. She came out of the lane in which her dorm was located. Haksh was standing near the lane. **The boy gave the food parcel to the girl.**

"What is there in it today?" asked Neha. "The parcel is big and a bit heavy"

"Go to your room and see what's in it? Inform me if the taste of the food is bad" said Haksh.

The girl took the food parcel and returned to her dorm.

"Haksh!" came a shout. Haksh turned back and found Madan.

"Hi Madan" said Haksh.

Madan was standing at one end of the railway tracks that were running below the over bridge. There were two railways tracks. Haksh was on the other side of the railway tracks. One could hear the noise of the train's horn. A train ran on the tracks. After the train left, Haksh crossed the two railway tracks and met Madan.

"Where did you disappear from the book fair? I was searching for you. **I even rang your phone number** " said Madan.

"Busy in some work" said Haksh.

"I have got something for you" said Madan. He gave a book to Haksh. The book was on Greek tales.

"This is a very exciting book." said Madan.

"Really" said Haskh

Madan gave the book to Haksh as a gift.

At the dorm, Haksh read the book. The book was on Greek tales. He was going through the tale of Pygmalion and Galatea.

"Galatea means milky white skin" Haksh read a sentence from the book. He stopped reading and looked at the wall in front of him. He shut his eyes. He remembered the face of Smruti for sometime then opened his eyes.

"I have seen a girl with milky white skin" said Haksh

to himself and smiled.

He read the book till late that night. He put the book on the table and went to his travel bag. He took out his purse from the bag. There was a photograph of Smruti in the purse.

"You are my Galatea" said Haksh and kissed the photograph before putting it back into the purse. The boy lay on his bed thinking of Smruti till sleep overcame him. She was his Galatea.

Chapter 24
The pygmalion

* * *

JANUARY, 2012
SAMBALPUR

The book fair ended, Haksh got a number of chances to walk all around the fair with Neha. Whichever book Neha wanted to buy, she got it with the help of Haksh. Both of them ate in cafes and roamed about the city. They even went to the cinemas to watch movies. The book fair ended, but there was no sight of Hemant. He was not coming to college to attend classes. One day while taking the roll call, the teacher called out the roll number of Hemant.

"He is absent" said Rocky, a student of the classroom.

"He has not come for a very long time" said the teacher.

Haksh felt sad about whatever had happened with Hemant.

After the classes were over he rang up Hemant and asked "Why are you not coming to college Hemant?"

"What is the use of going? When I go to college and see Disha then I go into mental depression. At home I am able to stay happy." said Hemant.

"I am sorry friend"

"You have already done the damage. Just as I am suffering, you too shall suffer." shouted Hemant and cut the phone. Haksh rang Hemant but the latter's phone was switched off. Haksh heaved a sigh. Hemant had cursed him. **Haksh** remained sad from that day.

"You are right Hemant." said Haksh while in his room in the dorm. He was looking at the photograph of Smruti in his purse. The face of the boy remained gloomy from that day. Madan marked this and asked, "What's the matter with you, Haksh?"

Haksh and Madan went to the stage near the PG hostel made for boys. They sat on the stage. Haksh told his problem to Madan.

"So, Hemant has cursed you" said Madan.

"Yes" said Haksh. "The boy is unable to realise that Disha is harmful for him"

"Do not worry he will realise it someday"

"But what about my problem ?" said Haksh . "I told you about Smruti. I just want her to feel my love"

"What? This is a very strange thing. People always try to dominate the other person, but you just want her to feel your love."

"Yes. I love her even if she does not respond to me"

"This is very one -sided"

"It may be one sided, but it is love."

"This is really very unusual."

"I do not have the **hope** of getting any response from her. I just have the determination to love her"

"Well, I think I have something that can help you"

"What's it?"

"Try to help some of your friends in their love lives. Help them celebrate with the ones whom they love. It may work"

"What kind of advice is it? Normally I hear people tell the other person to go for fairness cream, make up, do body building, etc"

"All those things are not permanent, but the act of

helping someone will make the other person help you or wish something good for you"

That whole day Haksh kept thinking about Madan's words . He did not go to college. He kept thinking about the whole thing while watching romantic movies on the laptop of his roommate in the dorm.

Chapter 25
Towards vikash

* * *

FEBRUARY, 2012
SAMBALPUR

Haksh went to college and entered the classroom meant for first year English Honours students. Madan came.

"Hey Madan" said Haksh. He shook hands with Madan.

"I am seeing you after a very long time. Where were you?" asked Madan.

"I was thinking about that suggestion of yours."

"Really? You remained absent from class for such a long time only to think about that suggestion."

"Yes. I have **remained** absent for some ten days. That's not a big deal."

"That means you love that girl a lot."

"That's why I have come to get some help from you."

"How can I help you ?"

"I am leaving for my hometown. You just keep track of whatever the teacher teaches in the classroom. I want this much help from you."

"Okay, that's not a problem"

After the classes were over that day, Haksh packed his bag and headed to the bus stand.

Nabin was standing at the bus stand. Haksh got

down from the bus with his luggage.

"What made you return?" asked Nabin.

"The summer of Sambalpur. It is very hot over there"said Haksh

This was true. The city of Sambalpur was experiencing a heat wave scorching it. Nabin started the bike and Haksh sat as the pillion rider. The brothers left the bus stand and reached home.

After reaching home,Haksh had bath, Mrs Namita served him watered rice and potato curry. The boy ate them heartily. Homemade food is always different from what one eats in the hotels. After eating , the boy went to his room and fell asleep. He was exhausted after the long journey.

......

JUNE , 2009

PADAMPUR

Haksh opened his eyes and stretched his limbs before giving a loud yawn. He came out of the bed and left the room. He had bath and wore a t-shirt and jeans. He packed his notebooks and put them in his backpack.

He rode his bike and reached an entrance gate on which it was written "ANCHAL COLLEGE".

Haksh was a student of that college.

MAY, 2009

PADAMPUR

Before the classes started at college , Haksh wished to see Smruti. He **went** to the playground on his bicycle. While cycling he looked at the roof of the building where Smruti lived. There was no sight of the girl. He asked Madhurja about Smruti.

"She has not come back from Bargarh. I have not seen her anywhere" said Madhurja.

"If you ever happen to see her,inform me" said Haksh.

At that time, Haksh's parents had not shifted their house from the town completely . They were waiting to see in which college the boy was going to do his higher secondary studies. After it was confirmed that Haksh would be doing plus two science at Anchal College, the family shifted to the village. The village was very far away from the town. Haksh could not go to the playground regularly due to the distance.

JUNE, 2009
PADAMPUR

The classes in Anchal College were very rigorous. Haksh had to remain updated in order to remain ahead of the rest students in the classroom and be the favourite of the teachers. He made two time tables for him.

TIMETABLE FOR WORKING DAYS:

> Go to college on time and attend the classes

>Return from college and revise what has been taught in the classroom

> Play a computer game

> Go to sleep after reading the letters that were to be given to Smruti and spend some time in thinking about her

TIME TABLE FOR HOLIDAYS

> Wake up and do some studies

> Maintain practical records

> Play computer games

> Go to sleep after reading the letters written for Smruti.

It was initially difficult for Haksh to follow the timetable but he got used to it with the passage of time. A life strained by routine is always helpful

.

MARCH, 2010
PADAMPUR

The first year of plus two came to an end. Haksh hadn't done anything path-breaking, but his score was not so bad either. Haksh heaved a sigh after seeing the mark sheet and said "Better luck next time. Try your best so that the score does not fall below the average mark."

After the first year plus two annual examinations were over, Haksh stayed indoors playing his computer game. One day his phone rang. It was Chinmay.

"Hello Chinmay!" said Haksh. "Nice to chat with you after a very long time"

"Haksh are your first year annual exams over?" asked Chinmay over the phone.

"Yes, it's over. What about yours?"

"It's over here too"

"That's good"

"When will your plus two second year classes start?"

"After a month"

"In that case I have an invitation for you"

"What for ?"

"The plus two second year classes are going to start very early in our educational institution, so I just want you to come here to meet me and some old friends from our school days"

"Inform me when you want me to meet you"

"I will inform you when our school reopens for classes"

"Okay"

Haksh agreed to go to Vikash Public School , which was located in Bargarh in order to meet Chinmay.

APRIL, 2010
PADAMPUR

One day Chinmay rang up Haksh and said "The school has reopened . The classes are going on. You can come"

"I will go tomorrow"

The next day Haksh left home on his bike. He told his mother that he was going to meet an old friend. The distance between Padampur and Bargarh is not much. If one goes speedily on bike then he will reach Bargarh within an hour. Haksh reached Bargarh and headed towards Vikash Public School. He reached the school, he halted his bike and waited for the school bell to ring. His cell phone rang. It was Chinmay who was ringing me.

"Hello, Chinmay" said Haksh.

"Haksh, have you reached the school?" asked Chinmay

"Yes" said Haksh. "How are you able to ring me from the school? Are you allowed to take cell phones into the school building?"

"I have not gone to school today."

"So, where are you now?"

"Just stay near the school. I am coming. Just give me ten to twenty minutes."

"Okay"

Haksh got down from his bike and parked it. He started playing a game on his mobile phone to kill the time. Chinmay reached the place and greeted Haksh. The two friends embraced each other.

"It is not yet the time for the children to come out. Let's go somewhere to pass the time" said Chinmay.

The two boys sat on the bike and left the place. They roamed about for some hours before returning to the school.

"Why have you called me?" asked Haksh.

"Wait for some minutes then you will know" said Chinmay.

The **gate** of the school opened. Haksh and Chinmay looked at the gate of the school.

"Keep looking at the gate of the school. Keep looking at the children who come out. You may find some familiar face" said Chinmay.

Chinmay and Haksh were standing some metres away from the entrance gate of the school. Haksh looked at the faces of the children coming out of the school. Suddenly his eyes became wide open.

It seemed as if he saw someone he knew in the crowd. He had spotted Smruti in the crowd of children who were leaving the school.

"Is that Smruti?" asked Haksh, unable to believe his eyes.

"Yes, it's Smruti" said Chinmay.

She walked in front of them. She did not look at them. She headed towards a car and got into it. The car left the place. Haksh was seeing Smruti after a very long time. He was unable to find words to express his joy. The boy took Chinmay to a hotel. Both the friends ate a lot.

.....

FEBRUARY, 2012
PADAMPUR

Haksh opened his eyes. The ceiling was visible to him. All this time he was having a flashback of an incident in his mind. He smiled to himself and got engrossed in playing computer games.

The next day, Haksh decided to go to the playground in the town to meet his old friends. While cycling towards the playground he saw the building where he used to see Smruti in the past. He halted his cycle infront of the building and stood still. He looked at the building and smiled.

Chapter 26
Morning walk

* * *

AUGUST, 2010
PADAMPUR

It was an afternoon. Haksh left home on his bicycle. He was passing in front of the building where Smruti lived. After entering the higher secondary stage of his career he had never seen Smruti in the building.

That day he was passing in front of the building when he caught the sight of Smruti. She was with a woman. The woman was holding a vegetable bag. Haksh got down from his bicycle and looked at Smruti and the woman. They entered the building. Haksh smiled.

He was seeing Smruti in Padampur after a long time.

....

FABRUARY, 2012
PADAMPUR

Haksh thought about that day and smiled a bit before getting on to his bicycle and heading towards the playground. He played with his friends. Chinmay was present in the ground. Haksh was overjoyed to see his friend. The two friends greeted each other.

FEBRUARY, 2012
PADAMPUR

The boys in the field were playing football. Haksh and

Chinmay joined them. After the game was over, Chinmay and Haksh sat on the grassy playground.

"Chinmay, have you seen Smruti anywhere in Padampur?" asked Haksh.

"No" said Chinmay

"A long time has passed since I saw her"

"Yes"

"Tell me if you see her doing morning or evening walk"

"Now, is that a joke or what?"

"Why?"

"I am remembering the days when you used to inform me about Smruti going for a morning walk and an evening walk."

The two boys laughed when they talked about some incidents in the past.

....

OCTOBER, 2010
PADAMPUR

Haksh was still a plus two student. He began to do rigorous exercise as he was thinking of making an attempt to go for the police service. He was cycling a lot in order to burn the fat that had accumulated around his thigh muscles. He would cycle from his village to the play ground in Padampur town. He would wake up very early and do cycling. Once while cycling near the playground he saw Smruti and her mother walking on the road. Haksh smiled at Smruti, but the girl did not look at him. In the evening when he cycled from the village to the playground to play, he saw Smruti once again. The next day he saw Smruti and her mother in the morning and in the evening . Every time the mother and the daughter were walking.

"She must be going on morning **walk** and evening walk" concluded Haksh. Now, he always came to the town in the morning and in the evening on his bicycle in order to see

Smruti doing morning walk and evening walk.

Once after playing in the playground Haksh and Chinmay were talking.

"Chinmay, can you tell me when does Smruti start her morning walk and evening walk?" asked Haksh.

"Why?" asked Chinmay .

"I am also thinking of doing a bit of walking with her"

Chinmay had the habit of going for morning walks and evening walks.He lived close to the colony in which Smruti lived. It did not take him much time to know the timing when the girl went for morning and **evening** walks. He informed Haksh about it. Haksh woke up very early and reached the town on cycle. He would park the cycle in the playground . There would be other people who would be doing exercise in it . After parking the cycle he would walk about in the neighbourhood of Smruti. Once he spotted the girl come out of the building with her mother, he would walk following them. He would follow them from a long distance. The mother and the daughter would go for a long walk. Haksh would walk up to some distance then return to the playground for his cycle. He would leave the town on the cycle. In the evening, towards five p.m he would reach the playground, park his cycle and follow Smruti and her mother for some distance when they would be taking their evening walk. This became a routine for Haksh until one day when he could not see Smruti anywhere. When Smruti and her mother were not visible for weeks together, Haksh felt that the girl had left the town.

......

FEBRUARY, 2012

PADAMPUR

"I have not seen her for a really long time" said Haksh.

"Yes, a very long time" said Chinmay.

The two friends talked about other things for sometime before leaving the playground.

Chapter 27
Help alok

* * *

FEBRUARY, 2012
PADAMPUR

After returning from the playground, Haksh was completely exhausted. He lay on his bed and fell asleep. It was late at night when he woke up. He had his supper and went to bed. He did not know from where to start his mission. He reminded himself of Madan's words. Madan had told him to help someone in love.

"Whom to help?" said Haskh to himself. He contacted Chinmay.

The two boys arranged a place to meet. One day they met in a hotel in the evening. Both ordered some delicacies that were made in the hotel and began to talk while eating. Haksh told Chinmay about his problem.

"So, you want to help someone in love, isn't it?" asked Chinmay.

"Yes" said Haksh.

"Why don't you help that boy Hemant? He is heartbroken"

"He does not like to see my face"

"When will you get time to play the game of Cupid?"

"I find it exciting"

"Will it be okay if you focus on cases where lovers

are in love with each other but are not getting a chance to meet?"

"Yes, that will do"

"In that case you can take the case of Alok"

"Alok ? Where is he? I have not seen him for a long time .Where is that girl with whom he was having an affair?"

"I will contact him. He is in town." said Chinmay.

Haksh returned home with a smile on his face. He had found someone whom he could help in love. He lay on his bed and began to think on various ways to help a person in love.

OCTOBER,2008
PADAMPUR

Once there was a kabbadi tournament among all the schools in Padampur. Haksh did not take part in the tournament as he did not know how to play the game. He had a friend named Sugyata who was enthusiastic in taking part in it. Haksh warned the boy about the hazards of taking part in the tournament because Sugyata had a frail body. Sugyata was insisting upon being a part of the kabbadi team. Haksh allowed him as he gave into Sugyata's stubbornness. Haksh went to the playground to see Sugyata play. Sugyata was playing for Town High School. In the match , Sugyata was sent to make a raid. The opposition players were successful in halting Sugyata from making a successful raid. He was floored by an opposition player and the rest jumped on him. He had to leave the field with an injury as all the players of the opposition team had pounced upon him.

"I had told you not to take part in the game. " said Haksh.

The opposition team was from another school in Padampur. The rivalry between the teams was limited to the field. After the match was over, a boy walked up to Sugyata and said "I'm sorry, for using all my force on you."

"You all would have killed me, Alok" said Sugyata.

"I was telling Sugyata not to take part in this game" said Haksh.

Alok looked at Haksh. They were seeing each other for the first time. Sugyata introduced Haksh to Alok. Alok and Haksh shook hands. This is how Haksh and Alok came to know each other.

MARCH 2009,
PADAMPUR

It was the vacation after the board examinations of class tenth. Alok was enjoying the vacation as he had cleared the class tenth board examination. He went to the mall to get a portrait. He was returning home when he met with an accident. Alok fell on the road. He stood up and found a girl standing near him. The girl was on a scooty.

"I am sorry" said the girl. Alok stood up from the ground and dusted himself. He looked at the portrait he was taking home. The portrait had fallen on the ground and had developed cracks on it. Alok looked at the girl and said "You broke that portrait. What's your name?"

"Why? Are you going to complain to my parents about this?"asked the girl

"Of course. You are unable to ride your scooty properly. You can kill someone someday" said Alok.

Alok held the handle of the girl's scooty. The girl was afraid.

" My.... my .. name is Swati" said the girl trembling.

"Where do you live?"

"In the colony nearest to the shopping mall"

"So, you live in my colony"said Alok. "Next time if I see you hit anyone on the road then I will surely inform your parents" added Alok and left the handle of the scooty. Swati started the scooty and left the place as fast as she could.

At night Alok got a phone call from Haksh.

"Did you have any accident today?" asked Haksh.

"Yes" said Alok. "But how do you know about it?"

"I was roaming around in your area in the afternoon . I halted near a small shop to get some mint chocolates. The shopkeeper told me about it"

"These shopkeepers of the colony know me and my friends properly"

"You are famous in your colony."

Alok narrated how the accident took place.

APRIL, 2009
PADAMPUR

Some days after the accident took place, Haksh and Alok were standing near a hotel and drinking soft drinks. Boys have the habit of roaming around a lot when they have no work. If they meet some friend while roaming, they would either eat or drink something with that friend. Haksh had the habit of roaming around on his cycle whenever he got some time. He was roaming in the colony near the mall when he met Alok. Both went to a hotel and ordered for two soft drinks. A group of girls entered the hotel. While talking with each other Haksh and Alok heard the girls giggle a lot. The two boys looked at the girls to see what was making them giggle. One girl got up from the group of girls and walked out of the hotel speedily. She sat on her scooty and left the hotel. The girls giggled even more after the girl left.

"Did you see the girl who left the hotel **on her scooty** ?" asked Alok.

"Yes" said Haksh.

"That's the one who hit me."

"Looks beautiful"

"I doubt if you would have given that remark had I been severely injured that day"

"She must be learning to ride the scooty."

"Yes. Her mother told me so."

"Mother? You have already met her mother?"

"Yes" said Alok "Her mother came to know about the accident from some source. She met me and said I did the right thing by shouting at Swati"

"What? The mother supported you?"

"The girl is very disobedient and she rides the scooty without any proper training. She deserved the shouting"

Haksh saw one kind of joy in the eyes of Alok when he was narrating the things linked to Swati. He doubted Alok had begun to nurture some feelings for that girl.

SEPTEMBER, 2009
PADAMPUR

The time for Ganesh Puja was coming closer. Haksh and his friends were collecting subscriptions from their locality for the puja. Haksh went to the colony in which Alok lived. Alok and his friends were collecting subscriptions in their colony. Haksh met Alok. Both of them were discussing on the preparations for the celebration of Ganesh puja in their respective colonies.

The boys were sitting in front of a tea shop. A group of girls passed in front of the tea shop .Swati was among the girls. Alok stopped speaking to Haksh and looked at Swati cross. The girls were on their scooties.

"What happened? Why are you looking at Swati?" asked Haksh.

"I see this girl a lot these days. I am beginning to feel something for her" said Alok.

"Just keep a good impression in front of her"

"Okay"

"Have you gone to their home to collect subscription for the puja?"

"Yes"

"Go to their home once again on the day before the puja"

"What for?"

"To invite them"

"Okay, okay"

"Be as a friend, smile at her, do not follow or do not do anything that makes her feel bad about you"

"Okay" said Alok. He thanked Haksh for the tips.

A few days after the Ganesh Puja was over the two boys met in the playground. Haksh asked about the puja celebration in Alok's colony.

"It was a fantastic" said Alok. "Swati came to see the puja decoration done by my friends and me"

"I see" said Haksh.

"I went to her home the day before the puja. I invited her parents to come to the puja. Swati was looking at me. Her parents have a good impression about me"

OCTOBER, 2009
PADAMPUR

As days passed, Alok reported Haksh about his meetings with Swati. The meetings increased as they lived in the same colony. Alok joined a college. He had to leave home early and return late in the afternoon after the college classes were over. Swati was studying in a college that was in the same town. They saw each other while going from the colony and while returning to the colony after their college classes. A time came when they shared their phone numbers. They shared their numbers when Swati was once again involved in a road accident. This time she hit her sooty against a car. The car's owner was going to take her to the police station. Alok intervened in the situation and eased **the owner** off. The man agreed to leave the girl if he was paid for the damaged rear **indicator** . He would not be going to the police station. This was a relief for Swati.

"You stay here. I am coming" said Alok to Swati. Swati had to stay with the car's owner until Alok returned with the money for the rear indicator . Alok went home and told his parents that he had hit the rear indicator of a car. His parents believed in him and gave him some money. The rear indicator of a car does not cost much. Alok paid the man and saved Swati from punishment. She was grateful to Alok for this.

"Keep my number in case you meet such accidents" said Alok. "You meet with a lot of accidents"

Swati smiled. Both of them shared their numbers. This led to a lot of text messaging, chatting , etc between them.

....

FEBRUARY,2012
PADAMPUR

Haksh was lying on his bed and thinking about the various ways by which he could help Alok and Smruti.

Chapter 28
Bizarre logic

* * *

FEBRUARY, 2012
PADAMPUR

While having a conversation with Alok, Haksh came to know Swati's birthday was coming. Haksh suggested Alok to surprise her with something.

"What do you want me to do? What kind of gift do you want me to give her?" asked Alok.

"She will celebrate her birthday with her parents on the exact day, but she will celebrate with you on the next day of her birthday"

"Now, how will that help me in my relationship with her?"

"Let me explain you my plan"

Haksh told Alok to invite the girl to a room that has all the things **that** she likes.

"We'll get a birthday cake. This will impress the girl." said Haksh

The boys started working on the plan. Alok used to have a lot of conversation with Swati over the phone. It did not take him much time to make a list of **the** things that she liked. Alok showed the list to Haksh. The boys ticked the ones which they could afford to purchase. The things they could afford were some teddy bears, some food items, some toys and a dress.

Haksh had a friend named Digvijay. His parents were in the railway so they had to move about from place to place. Digvijay lived in the house with three servants. Haksh and Alok met Digvijay in order to get some help.

"The cake would be placed in one room of the big building." said Haksh. The boys chose a room. Once they found a suitable room for the celebration, they decorated the room with decorative lights and other materials used for decoration.

On the day before the Swati's birthday Alok had a talk with her over phone.

"Happy Birthday to you in advance" said Alok over the phone.

"Thank you" said Swati, smiling.

"I have a surprise for you, but I will give that to you after your birthday"

"What's the surprise?"

"You will celebrate your birthday twice this month"

"Why?"

"You will celebrate your birthday anniversary with your parents and all your friends. You will celebrate **the** birthday anniversary once again in a place where only you will be present with your favourite things. No other human being will be there."

"That sounds interesting."

"That's why it's a surprise."

Swati's birthday **anniversary** came. Alok went to her home. **The girl** celebrated **her birth anniversary** with her parents and her friends. Alok and Haksh were in the party. Swati's parents had arranged a feast.

"The food is very tasty. Tell my thanks to Swati" said Haksh.

"Okay, I will" said Alok.

That day Haksh did not return to Padmapur. He

stayed at Madhurja's house. Madhurja was his cousin. The next day Haksh went to Digvijay's home. Digvijay and Haksh were busy in decorating the room for Swati. Alok reached Digvijay's residence in the afternoon.

"At what time is Swati coming **?**" asked Haksh.

"By five p.m" said Alok. Chinmay had come to the house to see the decoration.

The boys had arranged a big cake that had Swati's name written on it. There were some big teddy bears in the room and some lunch boxes that had Swati's favourite fast food **in them**. The boys began to wait for the girl's arrival. Alok was getting restless with each passing minute. The wall clock kept ticking. It was quarter past five but there was no sign of Swati.

"Have you shown her the house or not?" asked Haksh to Alok.

"Yes" said Alok. "I had shown her Digvijay's house from the road."

Alok called her over the phone but there was no response. The phone was switched off.

"Something has gone wrong. Let me call her mother" said Alok.

Alok rang to Swati's residence, but there was no response either.

"Don't ring to her home so much. It will be odd" said Haksh.

"Then what should I do?"

"Let us wait"

The boys waited up to eight in the evening. There was no sign of Swati. The girl's phone was switched off.

"It's late night. You go home." said Haksh to Alok. The latter was disappointed . **He** left Digvijay's house on his bicycle. Haksh and Chinmay decided to stay **at** Digvijay's house that night. The boys ate all the food that they had purchased for the celebration. The food would go waste if no one ate it.

Alok entered his colony. He was wondering why Swati did not show up that day.

"Let me got to her house and see what's the matter ?" said Alok. He went to Swati's home and found a number of people had gathered outside the house.

"Why are so many people outside the house?" said Alok. He saw an ambulance parked outside the house.

"What's the matter ? Why is there so much crowd here ? Why is the ambulance here?"He asked one person among the crowd .

"The girl named Swati met with an accident. Her dead body has been brought in the ambulance" said the man.

This was a bolt from the blue for Alok. He ran into the house and saw Swati's relatives crying inconsolably near her dead body. Alok burst into tears.

Haksh, Chinmay and Digvijay ate the big cakes and the fast food and went to bed. They came to know about the accident from Alok the next day. The boys went to Alok's home. Alok was devastated. He was crying inconsolably.

"How did it take place?" asked Haksh to Alok

"Swati met with a severe accident while on her way back from college. She was racing with her friends. They were on scooties. While driving speedily she lost control and hit against a lorry"

Haksh decided to leave Alok in his condition for sometime in order to allow the bereaved boy to come out of his pathetic condition on his own.

"Leave him in his condition for some time. He will come out of it" said Haksh to Chinmay and Digvijay in a low voice. The three boys left Alok's home.

"Swati had the habit of riding her scooty very speedily" said Haksh after reaching Digvijay's home . He had to do something with the teddy bears.

"Can I give these teddy bears to Elly?" asked

Chinmay.

"You can do whatever you like with them. The person for whom the bears were bought is no more" said Haksh.

Haksh left the Padampur town and reached home. He told his mother about **Swati's accident and Alok's condition** . Mrs Namita told him to have bath, eat food and go to bed. Haksh did as he was told. He had bath, ate some food and entered his room. He lay on his bed and waited for sleep to overcome him. He wanted to forget about the accident.

Swati's death was big shock for Alok. He would stay in his room all through the day remembering the moments he spent with Swati. Tears would roll from him eyes when Swati's memories would cloud his mind.

One night while sleeping he had a dream. In the dream he was **at** Digvijay's house. There was **the** cake meant for Swati on a table before him. There was a knock on the door. Alok opened the door. Swati was standing outside the door. Alok welcomed her and let her in. He took the girl to the room where the cake was kept. Swati cut the cake and gave a piece of it to Alok . He took the portion of the cake. He fed a part of it to Swati before taking a bite of it. Both of them began to eat the cake. There was no one in the house. It was like a moment of a lifetime for Alok. The boy was trying to live the moment. While eating the cake Swati's eyes went to the wall clock. She became serious.

"What happened?" asked Alok.

"You love me, no?" said Swati "Tell me the truth"

Alok was taken aback. He took some seconds to get back his composure and said"Yes, I do. But how did you know that ?"

"Seeing all this arrangement"

"That's too smart of you"

"Do not lose time. Get me the vermillion"

"What?"

"I want to be with you. Just do what I say. Get the red vermillion from anywhere and smear it on my head. I want to marry you"

Alok left the room and searched the house. He found a red sindoor box in the puja room of Digvijay's house. He returned to the room where Swati was waiting for him.

"Come with me" said Swati and held his hand. She took him to the puja room. Alok was in complete confusion.

Both of them stood before the portraits of the gods and **goddesses** in the puja room.

"Complete the work" said Swati. "I have no time. I have to go back"

Alok took out some sindoor from the small box and smeared it on Swati's forehead. The girl smiled. Tears came out **from** her eyes. She embraced Alok.

"Alok, I will be waiting for you" said the girl before disappearing into thin air.

....

Alok's sleep broke and he sat up on the bed. He had never had such a dream about Swati. He told Haksh about the dream.

"This is amazing" said Haksh.

MARCH, 2012
PADAMPUR

Two weeks had already passed since Swati died; Alok came out of his house for the first time. He wanted to shake off the grief.

He walked around the street and met his friends. He felt good. The next day he decided to go on a long drive solo. He rode his bike on the road that went to Bargarh. He liked the wind beating on his face. He increased the speed of his bike. There was a bus stop on the way. A small child came running onto the road. Alok applied sudden brakes to stop the bike from hitting the child. The **front** wheel of the bike slipped and he fell on the road. The head hit the road and he lost **his** consciousness.

Haksh was at home reading a book from his B.A. syllabus. A phone call came from Chinmay . Haksh was disturbed to know about Alok from Chinmay . Alok was being taken to Burla for medical treatment. Haksh wished Alok to regain his health, but that was not to be. Chinmay rang up Haksh in the evening.

"Haksh, I have a bad news for you" said Chinmay. "Alok is no more. He died due to severe head injuries due to the accident"

Alok's body was brought to Padmapur for funeral. Haksh was present at the funeral.

"He had told me about the dream where he spent some time with Swati. Alok must have left us to meet Swati" said Haksh to himself while looking at Alok's burning pyre.

Alok's memories began to trouble Haksh at home, so he decided to go to Sambalpur in order to mingle with his B.A classmates and forget the whole episode. There was another reason for him to return to Sambalpur.

One afternoon, he received a phone call from Neha.

"Where are you? Why are you not coming to the college?" asked Neha. "I have not seen you for quite a long time" she added.

"I am in Padampur." said Haksh.

"Did you leave the college? Are you studying anywhere else?"

"No, I am still a student of G.M College"

"I did not see you for a long time so I presumed you had left the college"

"But what made you ring me?"

"Nothing. No reason. I did not find you in the college for a long time, so I became curious to know what happened to you."

"Oh is that so?" said Haksh "How are the classes

going on?"

" The summer vacation is not far. The students are waiting for it"

"Thank you for the information"

"The vacation will end in the middle of June"

Haksh had a chat with Neha for a very long time. This made him feel light in the mind. He wanted to get rid of the grief of losing a friend.

"Alok went to his beloved. He is lucky to be united to his beloved Swati. My case is different. The girl I like does not even know that I love her. Smruti does not show any reaction to any action of mine." said Haksh to himself while packing up his travel bag. "So , it is wise to be with someone who is a lookalike of Smruti. In one way it gives the feeling of being with Smruti"he added.

He got into the bus and left Padampur. While in the bus he was reading **the** book that Madan had given him. It was on Greek tales. Haksh turned the page of the chapter that was on the tale of Galatea.

"I do not know how the girl you love looks like, but she is more or less like a Galatea- a girl who behaves like a lifeless statue towards your love for her. Do such action that life comes to the 'statue' and she begins to show human expression towards you" these were the words that Madan had told Haksh at college . While travelling in the bus, Haksh thought about Madan's words.

"Maybe my intention to help Alok led to the reaction of Neha calling me. She must be missing me a lot. The logic may be **bizarre**. Even if Neha is not Smruti, but she is like Smruti. This will do. Madan's logic is working" thought Haksh trying to believe in a **bizarre** logic. This may be **bizarre** but we all know the law of action and reaction that is universal.

Chapter 29
Computer classes

* * *

MARCH, 2012
SAMBALPUR

Haksh reached Samablpur and headed towards his dorm. He rang up Neha and informed her about his arrival.

"Where are you going for this computer course?" asked Haksh.

"It is an institution in Budharaja." said Neha over the phone.

"But where?"

"Okay I will show you in the evening"

"Okay"

Haksh slept in his room. He woke up after five thirty p.m and left his dorm wearing the best shirt and jeans. He rang up Neha and told her about his location. He was standing near the lane that had the "Shine Ladies' Dorm" in it. Neha came out of the lane with a notebook and a pen. Haksh smiled when he saw Neha. He walked with her up to the place where the computer courses were being provided.

Neha was to study in the building for one hour. Haksh waited for her near the building. After one hour the girl came out of the building.

"You are still here!" said Neha surprised to see Haksh.

"It's getting dark. I thought you might feel lonely

while returning to the dorm"said Haksh.

"Thank you"

Haksh and Neha talked a lot while walking towards the "Shine Ladies' Dorm". After Neha entered her dorm, Haksh headed to his dorm. Haksh escorted Neha to her computer coaching centre the

next day and the day after. It became a routine for him to take Neha to the coaching centre and **to** bring her back.

JUNE, 2012
SAMBALPUR

Time passed. March ended, April followed, and after that the summer vacations started in May. The month of June started. The exams of the second semester were to begin in the last week of June.

One day Chinmay rang up Haksh. He told Haksh to return to Padampur as soon as possible as there was an urgency. He did not tell Haksh what the urgency was. When Haksh insisted upon knowing what was the matter , Chinmay gave a hint by saying the urgency was related to Smruti. After hearing Smruti's name Haksh could not keep himself from going to Padampur. He went to Padampur by bus the next day.

Chapter 30
Meeting Uday

* * *

JUNE, 2012
PADAMPUR

Haksh reached home. His parents asked him why he came back. He said he had some work with Chinmay. He contacted Chinmay and said "Chinmay, I am in Padampur. Tell me about your important work."

"Meet me at the playground tomorrow" said Chinmay. "The one where we play cricket"

The next day Haksh reached the playground in Padampur-the one which was close to the Smruti's residence. Haksh met Chinmay.

"I have a great news for you" said Chinmay.

"What's it?" asked Haksh.

"Smruti had come to Padampur some days back" said Chinmay.

"What?"

"She had come with her family. Someone from their family got engaged. The marriage is taking place soon. May be this month"

"That means Smruti will be present in Padampur on the day of the marriage."

"She will be present in Padampur on that day."

Haksh wanted to have a glimpse of Smruti. Madhurja

was playing in the playground. After playing, he walked up to Haksh.

"Madhurja, can you tell me when Smruti is going to come for the marriage?" asked Haksh.

"This weekend" replied Madhurja.

Madhurja was a friend of Smruti's cousin. His name was Uday. Uday's sister was going to be married. Uday's father was Smruti's maternal uncle.

"Can we meet this Uday ?" said Haksh.

Madhurja helped Haksh meet Uday. He called Uday to the playground . Haksh and Chinmay met Uday.

"Will there be any problem if we attend the marriage ceremony?"asked Haksh.

"He is my relative. My father's sister is married to his father's younger brother" said Madhurja trying to explain his relationship with Haksh.

"Okay you can come. You are Uday's relative. I cannot call you a stranger"

Uday gave the invitation card of the marriage to Haksh. That night Haksh kept looking at the invitation card. "Urvashi weds Nikhil" was written in the invitation card. Urvashi was Uday's elder sister and Nikhil was **Uday's** would be brother- in- law. Haksh was looking at the invitation card as if he had got some ticket to meet Smruti.

Chapter 31
Bright dress

* * *

JUNE, 2012
PADAMPUR

Haksh went to attend Urvashi's marriage. He told his parents that he would be with Madhurja attending a marriage ceremony. His parents allowed him to go. The boy remained away from home for two days. On the first day, he went to Madhurja's home with Chinmay. There he waited for the evening to fall. Once evening came Madhurja , Chinmay and Haksh went to Uday's home. They entered the marriage ceremony by showing the invitation card to the security guards who were standing outside the gate. Urvashi's house had been decorated. There were some guests in the house. The courtyard had volunteers who were providing food service to the guests. Haksh , Chinmay and Madhurja were among the people moving about in Urvashi's house.

"How to find Smruti?" asked Haksh.

" She is yet to come. She has gone to a parlor" said Chinmay

"How did you know that?"

" I got the information from Uday."

"Does he know about the relation between Smruti and me"

"No"

"I am standing near the entrance and looking at the people who enter the wedding ceremony. Smruti will be coming by that way" said Haksh

"Okay"

Haksh kept standing near the entrance and looking at the guests. He waited for Smruti's arrival. He kept standing near the entrance gate and looking at the guests who were entering by the gate. Chinmay saw the condition of Haksh and felt sad. He walked up to Haksh.

"Will you be standing here all the time?" asked Chinmay

" I have no interest in the marriage ceremony. I have come here to see Smruti. I have not seen her for a long time." said Haksh.

A car reached the entrance gate, and Smruti came out of it. She was with her mother. They entered the entrance gate.

" Here comes my sweetheart !" exclaimed Haksh with a bright smile on his face. Throughout the marriage ceremony, Haksh kept looking at Smruti. She was in a bright dress.

Chapter 32
Kept Awake

* * *

JUNE , 2012
PADAMPUR

Smruti felt tired. Her mother took her to a room to sleep. The girl lay on a bed. The window of the room was open. Haksh peeped through the window and kept looking at Smruti's face. As it became dark, the lights were turned off, and the guests went to sleep. Haksh stayed near the window and kept looking at Smruti. The moonlight went through the window and fell on Smruti's face. Her face was glowing due to the moonlight and Haksh was looking at her as if he had been charmed.

"You fool what are you doing near the window instead of sleeping," said Chinmay in a low voice , when he spotted Haksh standing near the window.

" I am looking at Smruti" said Haksh.

" If anyone sees you then you will be beaten black and blue."

" Let me see my Smruti up to my heart's fill."

Chinmay left Haksh alone. Haksh kept standing near the window and looking at Smruti . When he felt tired, he left the window, but it had crossed midnight by then.

" A few more hours left for sunrise. Why waste that" said Haksh and continued watching Smruti from the window. The boy kept awake the whole night just to see the girl upto his heart's fill.

The next day, Urvashi left her home with the groom in a car decorated with flowers.After **the** bride left with the groom Haksh , Chinmay and Madhurja left Uday's home.

" Last night was the biggest night for me," said Haksh while driving the bike. "I could see Smruti up to my heart's fill. I kept looking at her for a very long time."

" I have some photographs of the marriage ceremony where Smruti didi is present," said Madhurja.

"That's excellent. I don't have words to thank you Madhurja," said Haksh.

Haksh got some photographs of the marriage ceremony from Madhurja and returned home. He went to **his** room and hid the photographs in a notebook.

Chapter 33
Unexpected attack

* * *

JUNE, 2012
SAMBALPUR

Neha was standing in front of the notice board. There were some students of G.M College who were standing in front of the main notice board. They were looking at the exam timetables that had been stuck to the notice board. Neha took out her notebook from her backpack and noted down the dates on which she had her exams. After noting down the exam a timetable of the Hindi Honours exam, she looked at the exam timetable meant for English Honours students. She rang up Haksh.

The second-semester examinations were going to begin towards the last week of June and end in the first week of July.

JUNE , 2012
PADAMPUR

"Hello," said Haksh responding to the phone. The boy was in Padampur market. He had gone for an outing. These days Haksh was rarely found at home. He was mostly found going on an outing. Sometimes he took some companion with him and sometimes he moved solo. This is the sign of a mind that is wandering. Haksh had become too overjoyed after the sight of Smruti. He was unable to focus on his lessons, so he was roaming around on his bicycle.

Now, coming back to the conversation with Neha. Haksh halted his bicycle and had a conversation with Neha over the phone.

"Why are you not coming to college. The exam timetable is out" said Neha.

" I am busy ," said Haksh.

They had a talk about preparations for the exam. Haksh asked Neha's help in preparing for Compulsory English and MIL Odia examinations. The girl assured help.

"Best of luck for the exams," said Neha.

"You too" said Haksh and ended the conversation. He sat on his bicycle and **started** pedalling. He went to an electronics shop, purchased a pen drive before heading home. He had to cycle a long way to reach home. It took him one to two hours to reach home on his cycle. The road to his village did not have too much human habitation. The boy was cycling comfortably when something hit his bicycle from behind. He fell on the ground. The next moment a group of boys circled him and beat him. They left him on the road after bashing him. This was an unexpected attack.

Chapter 34
Without thinking

* * *

JUNE 2012
PADAMPUR

Haksh kept lying on the road for some minutes before regaining his strength. He reached home and had **bath**. He entered his room and lay on his bed. He thought about the boys who beat him.

"Who were they? Why did they beat me?" thought Haksh.

He slept for a long time in the afternoon. After getting up he looked at the place where he had kept the photographs of Urvashi's marriage ceremony. He looked at the photographs. Smruti was present in all of them. Haksh smiled while looking at the photos, but when he saw one photo his smile disappeared. In that photo Uday, Urvashi, Nikhil, Smruti and another boy were standing together. Haksh looked at the face of the unknown boy who was standing with Smruti. He remembered the face of one of the boys who beat him that day. The face of the boy resembled the face of the one who was standing with Smruti in the photograph.

"So this boy beat me," said Haksh.

The other day he went to the town to meet Madhurja. He showed Madhurja the photograph and asked the identity of that boy.

" His name is Abhilash" said Madhurja. "He is Smruti's elder brother"

Haksh looked at Abhilash's photograph for as long time.

The moon was in the sky. Abhilash was riding his bike alone. A stone came flying and hit him on the head . He got imbalanced due to the impact of the stone on his face. He fell down on the road along with his bike. Before he could wake up a masked man ran up to him with a cricket bat. Like a batsman hitting a bowler, the masked man rained blows on Abhilash before running away .Abhilash was admitted to the hospital. His friends came to visit him. Haksh went to the hospital to see Abhilash.

"I don't get it. You beat him. Now, you are going to see him in the hospital" said Chinmay.

"To give a statement," said Haksh.

When Haksh came to know about the identity of the boy who beat him, he started to collect data about Abhilash. The day when Abhilash was beaten, Haksh and Chinmay were following him on the bike. The two boys had wrapped their faces with black clothes so that no one **recognised** them. They followed Abhilash on the bike. When they came close to Abhilash's bike, Haksh threw the stone forcefully at Abhilash.The latter was taken aback. He lost control of the bike and fell. Chinmay stopped his bike. Haksh got down from it and bashed Abhilash with the cricket bat before leaving the scene with Chinmay.

Haksh entered the hospital and saw Abhilash. He was lying on a bed. His head and his right hand were plastered. Smruti was standing near her brother. She looked at Haksh angrily. Haksh looked at her then at Abhilash.

"I have never misbehaved with anyone or forced my will on anyone," said Haksh looking at Abhilash. " The love of the lover may or may not get a response from the beloved , but that does not mean the heart of the lover will stop loving the beloved"

Smruti did not know what to say. She kept looking at Haksh

"Get well soon," said Haksh. He patted the shoulder of Abhilash then looked at Smruti before leaving the hospital. Chinmay did not understand what was all this for. Haksh did not tell him why he did all this. There was no time to think over the matter. Haksh left Padampur as he had to prepare for his semester examinations. He reached Sambalpur and headed to his dorm.

JUNE, 2012

SAMBALPUR

We do certain things without thinking, but later on, when we think about them we wonder why we did them. Haksh was in the same situation. He beat Abhilash out of anger, but after reaching

Sambalpur he kept thinking why did he beat the boy who was Smruti's brother.

"Smruti will never speak to me," said Haksh to himself while sitting on his bed in the room . " But she never spoke anything to me,"

Haksh was not interested in his lessons. The examinations were some five days away. He rang up Neha and asked if he could meet her.

" Have you kept **the** notes of Compulsory English and MIL Odia for me?" asked Haksh.

"Yes," said Neha.

"I will collect that from you this afternoon."

In the afternoon, Haksh reached the lane near the "Shine Ladies' Dorm" and rang up Neha. He waited for some minutes. The girl came out of the lane with some notebooks in her hand.

"These are your notes," said Neha handing over the notes to Haksh .

Haksh heaved a sigh and took them. Neha looked at Haksh's face and said " What happened? You don't **seem to be** happy ?"

"Exam stress," said Haksh . He lied. He was feeling sorry for beating Abhilash. He knew Smruti was going to hate him forever as he had beaten her brother.

" So much stress ?"

"Yes, I am very stressed for the exams.I feel I will not pass."

"Why won't you pass ? Study hard and you will get good marks."

" Well, let's forget about studies. We are meeting after a long time , so let's eat something."

Neha and Haksh went to a cafe and ate some food. While eating food Neha looked at Haksh. He looked thoughtful.

"You appear to be lost? Is your girlfriend behind it ?"asked Neha.

"No, not at all. I have no girlfriend," said Haksh with a start.

"Then why do you look as if you have some problem with someone you love."

"I have no lover. I am not in love with anyone" spoke the boy in a manner as if listening to the word love was hurting him like some nail. He looked in another direction to hide his angry face from

Neha. He was upset with himself.

" Okay sorry for raising the topic, but you should smile. You don't look good while brooding"

Haksh turned his face towards Neha and smiled. After eating the food in the cafe, he left Neha at her dorm before heading to his dorm.

Chapter 35
Food problem

* * *

JULY, 2012
SAMBALPUR

The second-semester examinations started. Haksh had to seek Madan's help during the exams. Madan went to the dorm where Gaurav lived. Haksh was living in Gaurav's room to prepare for the exams by discussion. Madan went to the dorm where Gaurav lived .He gave them the notes on the lessons that would come in the exam.

It was the season of rain and there was power cut. Gaurav's room became dark. The boys could not study. They decided to sit and gossip to pass the time. While talking Haksh's cell phone rang. It was

Neha's call. Gaurav's dorm was near the "Shine Ladies' Dorm". There was not much distance between the two dorms. This was the reason why Haksh was living in Gaurav's dorm as a guest. Haksh received Neha's phone call .

"Haksh , can I ask your help ?" said Neha.

"Yes, sure" said Haksh

"There is a power cut and it's raining. I have not made any food. Can you get me some food from outside ?"

Haksh' s eyes lit up as if he had cleared some job interview or as if he had found some hidden treasure. He stood up from the bed on which he had been sitting in

Gaurav's room.

"What do you want ?," said Haksh enthusiastically

" Any fast food." said Neha. " I am feeling hungry"

"Okay. I am getting fast food for you"

"It's raining . Let the rain stop" said Madan.

" No , I can't wait ," said Haksh and left Gaurav's room.

" Seems he has got some love interest," said Madan.

"He always stands on the roof of our dorm and looks at the **ladies'** dorm. He contacts a girl living in that dorm. She goes to the roof of the dorm then both of them look at each other and talk over the phone for long hours."

It was raining . Haksh did not care for it. He hired an auto rickshaw and reached a hotel . He ordered some fast food to be made. After the food was made and wrapped , Haksh carried the polyethene containing the food and left the hotel. Neha was in her room. She was looking at the rain from the window. The rain had not yet abated. Her cell phone began to ring. Haksh was **ringing to** her cell phone. She received his phone call.

" I am waiting for you outside your dorm," said Haksh.

"O dear you came in this heavy rain!"exclaimed Neha.

" You were hungry."

Neha ended the conversation over the phone . She ran out of her room and reached the ground floor. She saw Haksh standing outside the entrance gate .

"Do you know this boy" asked the watchman who was sitting near the entrance gate of the dorm.

"I had sent him to get me some food" said Neha. She walked up to Haksh.

"Take your food" said Haksh giving the polyethene bag to Neha.

" I am feeling so guilty for troubling you in this rain.

I am sorry" said Neha. She was blushing while apologizing. Haksh's attention was on her face.

"No need to feels sorry. Go and eat your food" said Haksh.

The girl entered her dorm. Haksh returned to Gaurav's dorm.

"So you came from the **ladies'** dorm?" asked Madan when Haksh entered Gaurav's room.

"Yes," said Haksh. " I gave her food" .

Haksh's phone began to ring. He took out his cell phone from his pant pocket.

"Neha is ringing me" said Haksh to his friends before pressing a key to answer the call.

"Hello Neha" said Haksh

" Haksh, did you reach your room or not?" asked **Neha**. She sounded concerned.

"Yes I have reached my room."

"Change your clothes and try to be warm. You may catch cold"

" Okay , I will do as you said."

" I am feeling guilty for making you go out in the heavy rain"

There was the sound of thunder . Haksh told the girl to end the conversation as it was not advisable to talk over the phone during thunder and lightning .**Neha ended the conversation over the phone**.

"Congrats you have impressed her " said Gaurav.

"And you wasted today's time meant for discussing lessons. That's very bad" said Madan

"Don't remind me of lessons" said Haksh to Madan as he sat on a bed. There were two beds in the room.

It rained for a very long time . Once the rain stopped, Madan took leave of Gaurav and Haksh and headed towards his home on his bicycle.

Chapter 36
With Neha

* * *

AUGUST , 2012
SAMBALPUR

Madan did not come to the dorm to discuss lessons with Gaurav and Haksh . He was busy with his lessons. He found Gaurav and Haksh lacking interest in lessons. Gaurav was mostly found moving around and Haksh was always busy with Neha. After the exams were over Haksh called Madan to a fast food shop under the railway over bridge.

"Come friend. Let us celebrate the end of the semester exam " said Haksh.

Haksh and Madan ate patties. While eating patties Madan asked " Haksh , why were you not serious about your lessons in this semester. I found you lacking interest in **preparing for the exam** , so I did not come to teach you ."

" I am bored of the lessons" said Haksh.

"Tell me what's the problem. What happened in the village? Why are you so much involved with Neha when you have your heart with Smruti?"

"Neha is a Smruti's look alike."

" Why are you giving a lot of stress on this lookalike of Smruti ? What happened to the real Smruti ?"

Haksh's cheerful face turned gloomy. He finished the patties and told Madan that he would be waiting outside the cafe. Madan finished eating the patties. He paid the shopkeeper and left the Shop.

" What happened, Haksh ?" asked Madan to Haksh.

Haksh told Madan about the incident that took place with Alok. Haksh was thinking of helping Alok and Swati, but both died. He even narrated what had taken place at Urvashi's wedding. Haksh got a chance to see Smruti , but her brother Abhilash beat him a few days after the wedding. Haksh got angry and beat Abhilash badly. The latter was taken to the hospital. Now, Haksh had no hope of making any impression in Smruti's heart anymore , so he was trying to spend time with Smruti's lookalike to forget Smruti.

"So you think , you can forget Smruti by staying with Neha?" asked Madan.

" I think so". **said Haksh**

" I don't think so."

"But I think staying with Neha is better than thinking about Smruti. Smruti does not show any response . I do not know how she feels about me. Either she should be angry, or she should smile, but she has no expression. She has no emotion like a statue. Neha smiles and talks **with** me."

"Hmmm... I think you have to take the right decision. At least Neha shows some reaction to you. You would have gone mad by going after that girl who does not show any emotion."

" Even if I am not with Smruti , I am happy to be with someone who looks like Smruti"

"That's amazing !"

The two boys laughed. Haksh saw Neha with her friends. They were drinking cold drinks at a grocery store. Madan saw Neha and allowed Haksh to go and be with the girl. The two friends said goodbye to each other and parted their ways.

After the exam was over the classes for third semester started. Haksh went to the class regularly but he found Madan was not coming to college anymore. Hemant never came to college to attend classes. He came to college only on the days of exam and on the days when the forms had to be filled up for the exam. Haksh did not think much about why Madan was absent . His attention was on Neha. She came to the college regularly.

In the second year of graduation, the students had to change some subjects among the elective subjects. Haksh's name was among the students who had taken Education as their elective subject . He was happy to find Neha to have taken the same subject. Both of them met whenever they were in the Compulsory English classes and Education classes . They became close friends. They began to stay in the college after the classes were over. One day Haksh decided to give the girl a sign that he was in love with her. He called the girl to a hall. The girl came. She had a notebook in her hand. She sat on a bench and began to copy something from one notebook to another. She was so engrossed in copying that she forgot the presence of Haksh. The boy was sitting to the left side of Neha. He took his face close to Neha's left cheek. After writing a lot , Neha felt the back of her neck ache.

She shook her head from left to right to get rid of her ache. When she shook he head to her left her cheek touched Haksh's lips. Neha was taken aback.

"What are you doing ?" said Neha, taken aback.

" For some days I have been trying to suppress my thoughts. I decided to tell you what I felt for you . I love you" said Haksh.

Neha was left speechless for some **seconds**. She looked straight at Haksh before lowering her head and blushing.

"What are you saying ?" said Neha.

" Is there any problem ?" asked Haksh.

No word was shared between the two for several minutes. Neha did not know what to say. She was unable to decide what to do. Whether to leave the hall or to stay with Haksh ?

"Speak. Say something." said Haksh.

"I do not know what to say. My parents will not let me" said Neha.

" See whether you love me or not is not at all my botheration. I love you . Even if you do not love me, I will love you" said Haksh.

Neha was unable to find words to say. She decided to leave the place.

"Give me some time," said Neha as she put her notebooks in her backpack.

"Okay," said Haksh. Both of them left the hall. They did not speak to each other for a week. Haksh told Gaurav about what he had done.

" Wait for her response," said Gaurav.

Haksh became impatient. He rang up Neha. She picked up the phone.

" Neha, what did you think about me? What was your decision?" asked Haksh over the phone .

" I don't know what to say." said Neha, trying to check her smile.

" Okay you take your time. Listen here . I have to say something."

"What's it?"

" I have not met you for a long time. I miss you very much . Let us go for some sightseeing."

" I will not go to places that are very far from the college. I will not go alone."

"You won't go alone . You will have other people to accompany you."

"Who all?"

" You will see that day after tomorrow," said Haksh.

Haksh told Gaurav about his plan to visit a nearby temple. Guarav called Sandhya to meet him day after tomorrow. On the fixed day Haksh was waiting for Neha . Gaurav called Sandhya over the phone . The girl reached his dorm in the afternoon.

Haksh and Gaurav came out of the dorm.

"Sandhya you have to meet a girl named Neha. She is a student of Hindi Honours," said Gaurav to Sandhya.

Sandhya entered the Shine Ladies' Dorm and came out with Neha. Haksh had informed Neha about Sandhya the previous day.

After coming out of the dorm, Neha asked Haksh , "Where are we going ?". Haksh said they were going to the nearest temple of Sai Baba. The boy was trying to forget his troubled affair with Smruti by being with Neha.

There was a temple of Sai Baba in a lane of Budharaj. Haksh, Gaurav , Neha and Sandhya went to the temple on foot. Once they entered the temple, they burnt earthen lamps and offered their prayers before heading towards the park that was a part of the temple property. One speciality of the park was that it was open only in the afternoon . This restriction was put to keep the park clean because

we Indians have a habit of creating a mess in any park that we go. Only Haksh, Gaurav, Neha and Sandhya know what they did in the park and how they spent the time in it . They left the park towards five p.m. Neha went to her dorm, Sandhya rode her scooty and went to her home and the two boys went to a grocery shop to purchase some eatables . That night Haksh did not stay at Gaurav's **dorm**. He returned to Hridayam Boys' Dorm.

"You are returning to your dorm after so many days" said Mahesh when Haksh entered the room.

"I was in Gaurav's room to spend the time" said Haksh.

The intimacy between Haksh and Neha grew with each **passing** day. They stayed in the college after the classes were over, they would move around the town , go to movies and go sightseeing. Neha had

a relative who was pursuing a post graduation degree in the college. He spotted Neha's activities and informed her father about it. One day Neha met Haksh in the hall in the college. That day she was **looking very** sad. Haksh asked the reason.

"Someone told my father about my activities," said Neha.

"So what did your father say?" asked Haksh.

"He told me to study properly or else **he will get me married** ."

" Who informed him about your activities ?"

" There is one fellow named Pradip who is doing his post graduation in the Department of Political Science."

Haksh began to collect information about Pradip. He met the boy in the college playground . Both had a conversation. Haksh came to know a number of things about Neha. These were things that Neha kept hidden from him.

Chapter 37
Genuine case

* * *

AUGUST , 2012
SAMBALPUR

Gargabh lived in Bargarh. Once Gargabh was at his home. Neha's relatives called him and his father. They were invited to a lonely place to settle the issue about what all things had taken place with Neha. Once Gargabh and his father reached the place, Neha's relatives beat them. From that day Gargabh hated Neha .

Haksh learnt about this incident from Pradip. After a few days he began to receive phone calls from an unknown number. The caller gave him threats for having relationship with Neha.

Haksh informed Nabin about what had taken place **at college**.

"We sent you to study , but you involved yourself in some kind of trouble " said Nabin.

"Sorry ,Brother," said Haksh.

Once Neha's father and her brother had come to the college to see who this Haksh was . Haksh was standing near a shop outside the college boundary. He was with Gargabh. Gargabh spotted Neha's father and her brother. He informed Haksh about them. Haksh looked at Neha's father and brother from a distance. The father and the son duo looked at Haksh and left the place on a bike. **Haksh got phone calls from the unknown person who claimed to be Neha's relative.**

" Meet us to settle the matter, or else we can even file an FIR against you" said the person.

Haksh informed his brother about his problem .

" Tell them that you are ready to meet" said Nabin.

Haksh rang to the unknown person and said he was ready to meet Neha's family.

"Meet us this Saturday near the cinema hall in Bargarh," said the stranger.

AUGUST 2012,
BARGARH

It was night .There was no one moving on the streets. Haksh was standing infront of the gate of the cinema hall in Bargarh. He rang to the person who always rang him and said " I am waiting near the cinema hall."

After a few minutes, some auto rickshaws halted near the cinema hall, and some people came out of it armed with sticks. These were Neha's family members and some of their friends.

" They are coming . Be ready" said Haksh over the head phone that he had inserted in his ears. He removed the head phone and walked towards the armed people.

"What did you do to my daughter ?" demanded a middle- aged man . Haksh guessed that it could be Neha's father.

He did not respond to the man and ran away.

Neha's family members chased him. Haksh led them upto a place where Nabin was waiting with friends. Neha's family members and their friends had not anticipated this. A street fight broke out. Neha's family members and friends were beaten by Nabin and his companions.

SEPTEMBER, 2012
SAMBALPUR

Haksh came to college as usual. Now, he began to ring to the stranger who used to give him threats about Neha's father being a very bad person , etc.

"Will you call me once again to meet Neha's father?" asked Haksh to the stranger over the phone, teasingly. "No, sorry . It was a mistake ," said the stranger and cut the phone.

Haksh kept ringing to that stranger until the stranger stopped using that SIM number . Whenever he saw Neha in the college , he would pretend to be talking to someone over the phone and shout ," Partner, do you need any girlfriend.? Tell me if you want. I can arrange one readymade item for you."

Neha would hear this and walk away quickly. She knew whom Haksh was referring to . Tears would well up from her eyes whenever she heard Haksh pass indirect comments on her in the college.

Haksh had not told anyone about the way he and his brother had beaten Neha's relatives .

One day Madan caught sight of Neha crying and Haksh passing comments on her. He asked Haksh what the matter was . Initially, Haksh was reluctant to tell anything , but Madan insisted to know what had happened . Haksh told him everything.

"You beat Smruti's brother. Now, you beat Neha's father and her brother. This is a great thing." said Madan. "All girls will be afraid of you if you keep beating their relatives."

" Neha was a cheat. She looked like Smruti , but she was not like Smruti in behaviour ."said Haksh.

"I think you must help Hemant in his problem. That boy has cursed you . The curse was sincere ; that's why you are suffering such bad luck" **suggested Madan**.

"Even I think so . Hemant is terribly upset with me. After that day he stopped talking to me."

" I used to think there was no problem in ignoring Hemant , but after seeing the events taking place with you , I think you should do something for **that** boy."

The two boys concluded that they should help Hemant as he was a genuine case of a boy in love needing help.

Chapter 38
Ayurvedic college

* * *

OCTOBER , 2012
PADAMPUR

It was the month of October. The Dushera holidays started. Haksh was back at home. At home, the **Haksh's family members** discussed about his activities in G.M College. Nabin would make jokes on Haksh's relationship with Neha.

" The girl was very beautiful , but every beautiful girl is not so beautiful at heart." said Nabin to Haksh when the two brothers were having breakfast.

Haksh did not say anything . He just smiled.

"So, what are your plans for this Neha . **Are you** going meet her in college after the holidays are over?" asked Nabin.

"Brother, don't make such jokes on that matter ,"said Haksh.

" It was a very lovely affair."

" Nabin, do not add salt to Haksh's wounds.He is trying to forget that girl, " said Mrs. Namita.

" Maa, tell brother not to remind me of that matter . I want to forget it ," said Haksh.

Haksh spent the Puja Holidays by moving about the town on his bike. The family had three two-wheelers. Mr Bijay

, Nabin and Haksh had their bikes. The income of the family had increased because now Nabin was also earning money by working as a **contractor . Haksh** was missing Smruti a lot. He wanted to know where she had gone. He rang up Chinmay. The latter was in Padampur to spend his holidays. Both the friends met in the playground in Padampur.

On previous occasions they used to play with the boys in the playground, but that day they sat on the grass and looked at children play.

"Time flies very fast. Some years ago we were playing on this playground ," said Haksh.

"Why are you talking of time ? What's the matter?"asked Chinmay.

" I am missing Smruti ," said Haksh.

"I have not told you one thing because you might feel bad,"said Chinmay.

"What?"

"Smruti was my classmate in the Ayurvedic college"

Haksh heaved a sigh and slapped his head out of disappointment when he heard the name of the Ayurvedic College.

Chapter 39
A counselling

* * *

JUNE,2011
PADAMPUR

After the plus two examinations, Haksh was waiting for the results to come out. The results were to come out after a month. When the results came out , he went to an internet cafe to check his score. He was operating a computer and checking the results. He had scored something between seventy and eighty percent in the plus two **board examination**.

"Let me check Smruti's marks," said Haksh to himself. He had got Smruti's exam roll number from Chinmay. Chinmay was Smruti's classmate in plus two. Haksh entered Smruti's roll number and checked her marks. She had got some two to three percent below him.

"I have got more than her," said Haksh and smiled. He got a print out of his mark sheet and left the computer. He saw Smruti in the cafe. She was with her father. She saw Haksh and then turned her face in another direction to pretend she had not seen him. Haksh smiled at her before leaving the cafe.

After the plus two results are out , students try to fill the online admission forms of various colleges for their graduation level of studies. Haksh and Chinmay filled the forms of different colleges.

Haksh filled the online admission form of G.M College , which is a celebrated college in the western **region** Odisha, and submitted it . Haksh, too, filled the admission form of the Ayurvedic college . The last day of submission of the hard copy of the admission form in the case the Aryurvedic college was too far . Haksh did not bother to submit the hardcopy of the form as he thought there is no need to hurry as the last date was very far. When the list of the names of the students who had got admission in GM. College came out Haksh was delighted to see his name among the list of the students who were going to study English Honours. Before the beginning of B.A classes a counselling is done. Haksh went to **G.M College** for his counselling and forgot everything about the **admission** form of **the Ayurvedic College**. ....

OCTOBER, 2012
PADAMPUR

Now, when Chinmay told him about Smruti studying in Ayurvedic College, Haksh felt sad. He thought about the forgotten **admission** form.

" Even I could have got a seat in the college had I submitted the admission form," said a sad Haksh.

"What has happened to you? No need to keep thinking about it" said Chinmay to cheer up Haksh.

"But I could have been her classmate in the **Ayurvedic College**."

"Stop thinking about that matter and watch the children play"

The two boys remained silent and looked at the boys playing in the playground.

Chapter 40
Some suggestions

* * *

OCTOBER, 2012
PADAMPUR

The sun went down, and the children began to leave the playground. Haksh and Chinmay stood up from the grass and left the playground.

Haksh told Chinmay about Neha and all those things that had taken place in G. M College .

" You want to help that boy named Hemant, right?" asked Chinmay.

"Yes," said Haksh. " But I do not know how to help him . The girl he loves is a whore"

" You should never call a girl a whore."

" I have respect for girls , but I have no respect for a girl who keeps sleeping around with different boys."

" Hm.... , I feel Hemant has been hurt by you . Maybe that's the reason you to are facing a lot of problem in your private life."

" It could be ,"

"Why don't you come to Bhubaneswar to refresh your mind?"

"Where will I stay in Bhubaneswar?"

" In my dorm"

"Your dorm?"

" I have left the Ayurvedic College in Padampur and

joined an Ayurvedic College in Bhubaneswar."

" When are you moving your belongings from here ?"

" I have already shifted . I left this college and joined that new college in August."

" That's good . **You** will get new job opportunities in the capital city."

The two boys rode their respective bikes and left the place.While riding Chinmay said " Haksh , can you tell me everything about Disha ?."

"Why ?" asked Haksh.

"Normally, when a boy finds a girl to be sleeping around **with different boys** he leaves the girl , but Hemant is after the girl even after knowing everything about her. It is the girl's misfortune that she is unable to understand the boy."

"I will tell the matter to you over the phone. Let me reach home. My parents will be worried if I am late" said Haksh before bidding goodbye to Chinmay. Both were going to discuss on Disha and Hemant over the phone. Haksh was happy to find someone who could give him some suggestions regarding the problem.

Chapter 41
Long chat

* * *

NOVEMBER, 2012
SAMBALPUR

The Dushera holidays were over, and the students had to come back to **the** college to attend their classes. Haksh had to leave home to and return to his dorm. **Chinmay had to leave Padmapur and go to Bhubaneswar for his classes.**

Hemant came to college. The third-semester examinations were going to be held after a few days. The students were going to classes to clear their doubts and do some final revision with the teachers.

Haksh entered the class. The teachers told the students the various important sections of the syllabus from which important questions were to be expected. After the classes were over Hemant was heading towards the cycle shade.

"Hemant" called Haksh.

Hemant could recognise the voice . He did not stop walking. Haksh increased the pace of his steps and caught up with Hemant. He held Hemant's hand.

" Hemant stop," said Haksh.

Hemant halted and looked at Haksh with anger.

"Stop for what?" demanded Hemant.

Madan reached the spot and said " Hemant, we have

a solution to your problem."

"Which problem?" asked Hemant looking at Madan

"Don't pretend to be ignorant. You are upset with us because of Disha" said Madan.

" I don't think that girl will ever talk **with me**," said Hemant , heaving **a sigh** of disappointment.

" Don't be disappointed . That won't be the case anymore," said Haksh

"What?" said Hemant , surprised.

"Yes," said Madan.

That day Haksh , Hemant, and Madan went to the Trust Fund hostel. They went to Gopal's room. Gopal was busy with his books while the three boys were busy in a discussion. As the discussion progressed, Hemant became curious and excited. He was going to make an attempt to contact Disha after a very long time . **He left the hostel with confidence** . He left for his home on his bicycle. On the way home he halted near a shop that recharged phones. He recharged his cell phone with a big amount .

The boy was going to have a long chat with Disha.

Chapter 42
A leftover

* * *

NOVEMBER, 2012
SAMBALPUR

Disha was in her room . She was trying to help her uncle's children in their lessons. The girl used to read her own books then assist the children in preparing their lessons for their exams . She heard her cell phone ring. The girl took out the phone from her college bag. Hemant's name appeared on the screen of the phone.

"Why is this boy ringing me ?" she wondered. She did not respond to the phone call and put the cell phone back into the bag.

She continued teaching the children . **Her cell phone vibrated**. She took it out from her bag . This time a text message had come from Hemant.

" I want to talk to you. Please make some time. I have not spoken a word or done any kind of nuisance for a long time. I have to say something" Disha read Hemant's text message . This time she thought for sometime before sending a reply.

"Okay wait" typed Disha on **her** cell phone and sent a text message to Hemant. There were no further phone calls from Hemant after the text message was sent. Disha taught the children. After nine **O' clock** at night Disha's uncle and aunt and their children slept. Disha was alone in her room. She gave a missed call to Hemant. The boy had been waiting for the signal. His parents had slept . He locked the door of his room from inside before ringing to Disha.

" Hello Disha" said Hemant

"Yes, say" Disha. "Why did you ring me? How did you dare to ring me ?"

" I was feeling very restless"

" Let me make it clear. I am not in love with you and I will never nurture any such feelings for you"

" I do not have **any** interest in the leftover of someone else"

"What? What did you just say?"

"I have no interest in the leftovers of other people, so never think that I will show any such interest in you. The place of a leftover is always in the garbage bin where dogs gather to eat ."

Disha was left shocked by whatever Hemant told her over the phone. She had never expected this from Hemant. For her Hemant used to be a docile boy , she never expected the boy to address her as a leftover.

Chapter 43
Welling up

* * *

NOVEMBER, 2012
SAMBALPUR

Disha wanted to end the conversation abruptly and switch off her phone , but Hemant warned him from doing so.

" Don't even think of such things or else I will tell your uncle and aunt about your activities in the college. If they know what you do in **the college , then** you can imagine what will happen to your student life in the college," warned Hemant. " It won't take time for me to collect proof against you because all those boys with whom you had relationships are my friends. So, you have to listen to whatever I say."

"What's the matter ? Why are you behaving in this way to me?" asked Disha.

"Because I am fed up."

"Of what?"

"Parents expect something from their children. Your parents sent you here to study. They must be having very high hopes, but **what are you doing ?** First you were with Gopal , then you were with Gaurav and after that with a number of boys "

" I am with Gaurav. He loves me ."

"Some days back you had a chat with him , isn't it ?"

"Yes, I did . So, what's your problem?"

" Gaurav is already in a relationship with another girl. Her name is Sandhya . What do you want to prove by keeping physical relationships with Gaurav ? Neither does he want to settle with you nor does he want to be with you. You always force him to do physical contacts with you. Even in the case of other boys , I have found that they already have their lovers , but they use you to pass the time.

Why do you behave in this way ?"

"What? It's a lie."

" Don't cheat me. I know what you do with Gaurav and other boys in the halls of the college after the classes are over. It is not a case of one or two days but of several days."

"I have not done anything. It is the boys who force me to go to hall and have physical relationships with them. "

"Why should I believe in you? All those boys are my friends .And I know them properly. You are a lowly girl. Very cheap."

Tears were welling up from Disha's eyes. Hemant's words were hurting her like blows from a hammer.

Chapter 44
Good night

* * *

NOVEMBER , 2012
SAMBALPUR

Hemant knew Disha was on the back foot after listening to whatever he said. He did not want to lose the opportunity to take out his frustration on her.

"Why are you silent? Where is your anger? You used to turn your face away from me . Proud people turn their face away because they can, but what kind of pride is there in having physical relationships with a number of boys who are already committed to others?"asked Hemant.

"No, I have not done anything. Gaurav forced me to do that. He pulled me to **the halls**. The boys forced me to do that."

" Leave it. I heard from him and the other boys that you were saying a lot of things against me. For you, I was a bad boy because I spoke ill of you. I always criticised you, I always misbehaved with you. I admit my mistake . But tell me how can I respect a girl like you ? If you would have been someone's wife then I could have respected you; if you would have remained committed to one lover then I would have respected you , but how can I show respect to a girl who is keeping physical relationships with a number of boys ?"

" I have not done anything. I have not done anything"

pleaded Disha.

"**Why are you pleading to me ?** Do you know **how much you have** hurt me ?" said Hemant. " I kept loving you all this time. If you had stayed committed to someone else , I would have been happy remaining as your friend or as your lover's friend . For me, love is not about kissing and embracing the beloved, for me it is about being happy in the presence of the person you love, enjoying the beloved's smile, trying to spend time with her or to help her when she is facing a crisis. For me, even friendship is a form of love."

Hemant could hear Disha sulking.

" Disha... Hello, Disha..... Are you listening to me ?" said Hemant.

" I ....m.. I...am...sorry..." said Disha in a choked voice. Tears were rolling down **her cheeks . " I am very sorry.. for hurting you so much."she added**

" I asked you every time to make me at least your friend, but you remained hostile. Do you think I would have ever done all those things with you which Gaurav and other boys have done ? Do I look that evil ?"

" No. I was just carried away by my friends. I used to see them moving about and make boyfriends , so I was trying my luck."

"But now you might have realised your mistake. Just image what will happen to you if your parents come to know about you ?"

" Listen here."

"Yes."

" I do not want to talk about it. Please do not mention about it ever."

" Okay I won't, but I have a condition,"

"What's the **condition?"**

"I hurt you a number of times by calling names when you were with other boys . Will you forgive me and just be my friend ?"

" Okay I forgive you. But do not do any nuisance with me."

" You forgave me but what about friendship."

"Okay you will be my friend. But keep in mind you will only be my friend. Never try to exceed it"

" Thank you. For me, even friendship with you is a big thing," said Hemant. " Now, please smile."

Before ending the conversation over the phone Hemant and Disha said good night to each other. Hemant lay on his bed with a bright smile on his face. He was smiling after a very long time.

Chapter 45
Recent development

* * *

NOVEMBER, 2012
SAMBALPUR

The next day when Haksh entered the college premises, he saw Hemant running towards him. The boy embraced Haksh tightly.

"Thank you, friend. Thank you for the idea you gave me" said Hemant.

"What happened ?" asked Haksh breaking the embrace.

" Disha was sad for whatever she had done. She accepted me as her friend."

"That's great."

"But she warned me that she would see me only as a friend and I should not cross the line of friendship."

"Sometimes it is better to remain as a friend with the person you love. At least she does not hate you" said Haksh. "That's the plus point."

" Yes, thank you for giving me another definition of love. We think love is complete only when the other person responds to us with love or moves around with us or kisses us . You changed my thought about it. Now, I think love means to be with the one you love in some way or the other. If not as a lover then as a friend. The joy is not in her loving you , but in you being with her and she feeling happy being with you in any form "said Hemant and again embraced Haksh.

" Calm down . Calm down , friend. Your task has just begun" said Haksh.

Haksh told Madan about what had happened between Hemant and Disha the previous night. Madan was happy to know Hemant was able to befriend Disha. That day Hemant told Haksh and Madan to stay for sometime at Gopal's room in Trust Fund Boys' Hostel. Haksh and Madan waited for Hemant in Gopal's room in the hostel. Hemant returned with a polythene bag which contained three plastic containers that contained noodles .Hemant was giving a treat to Madan and Haksh. The three boys ate the noodles. Gopal was in the room. He came to know about the recent development that had taken place between Hemant and Disha.

" Hemant, you should have got something for Gopal. He is our classmate. Both of you were in love with Disha" said Madan.

Hemant opened a chain of his backpack and took out another polythene . It contained samosa and chutney. He gave the polythene bag to Gopal saying " This is for you."

"All the samosas for me ?" asked Gopal.

" I will eat them with you," said Hemant.

"I will also eat with you two," said Haksh.

Madan ate the noodles and left for his home . Haksh , Hemant and Gopal ate the samosas and the noodles. While eating Haksh asked " Gopal, are you still in touch with Disha?"

"No, I left her . I am now having a good friendship with Jyoti," said Gopal. Jyoti was Gopal's classmate in the college.

" Good," said Haksh. " Hemant, now you should focus on your studies.Do not contact her .Wait for the new year to come."

"Okay," said Hemant.

DECEMBER, 2012
SAMBALPUR

The third semester exams started. After the third semester exams was over , the students studying in the second year of English Honours got some holidays. Their classes were going to resume towards the first week of January. After the third semester was over, Haksh returned to his village to relax.

Chapter 46
Greeting card

* * *

JANUARY, 2013
SAMBALPUR

The new year came. The results of the second semester examinations , **which were held in** the month of June the previous year, were to come out towards the weekend of the first week of January.

Disha went to the college on the weekend to see her results. She was happy to see her marks . She had got first class in her Honours paper. After looking at the result on the notice board, she went to the examination section to get her mark sheet.

In the college, a wall **protected the plants** planted for **the Department of Botany**. Inside the wall there are plants, and outside the wall, **were the** bikes and bicycles of the **students**. Disha had parked her cycle near the wall. When she returned to her bicycle with her mark sheet , she found a colourful polythene bag hanging from the handle of the cycle. She removed the bag from the handle and saw its content. It contained a large colourful card. It was a New Year greeting card for her.

"Wow" exclaimed the girl on seeing the card. It was big and beautiful. She looked at the name of the sender. It was Hemant. She rang up Hemant from the college.

"Hello , Hemant , where are you ?" asked Disha over the phone.

"At home" said Hemant.

"Didn't you see your marks?"

" I saw my marks and returned home."

" Thank you for the greetings card."

"Welcome."

The next time when Hemant went to college, Disha met him after the classes were over. She gave him a New Year card.

"Thank you" said Hemant looking at the card in his hand.

Disha was standing in front of him with a smile on her face. Haksh and Madan were looking at Hemant from a distance. Disha left after giving the card. Haksh and Madan walked up to Hemant . They saw the card in Hemant's hands.

" Thank you, friends, for all this," said Hemant to Haksh and Madan.

" Welcome ," said Haksh. "After seeing you in grief, I made it my objective to make you happy."

Hemant thanked Haksh and left the place.

" Hemant is happy , so what do you think about it ?"asked Haksh to Madan

"Think what?"

" I made a lovelorn fellow like Hemant happy . What about my love?" said Haksh

"Let the fourth semester examinations be over then you will think about that question. I know you must be feeling lovelorn ."

" I have not got any chance to see Smruti for a very long time."

" Let the fourth semester be over."

MARCH, 2013

SAMBALPUR

The fourth semester was going to be held in the

month of March. On the days of exam, Disha would go to a hall and sit alone . She would do her last minute revisions in the hall before going to the classroom to take her exam. **One day Haksh** saw her in the hall. An idea occurred to him .

Chapter 47
Redeemed himself

* * *

MARCH, 2013
SAMBALPUR

On the exam days , Haksh , Gaurav, Madan and Hemant would go to Gopal's room in the Trust Fund Hostel. The boys would be busy doing last minute revision of the lessons. On one exam day, Haksh told Hemant about Disha doing last minute revision in a hall. Hemant was overjoyed. He left the room and entered the college building. He entered the hall where Disha was doing her revision.

Disha was surprised to see him.

" Best of luck," said Hemant.

"You too,"said Disha breaking a smile .

"You look very beautiful today"

"Thank you," said Disha ,lowering her eyes and blushing.

Hemant left the hall with a bright smile on his face. That day after the exam for the day was over Haksh , Hemant , Madan, and Gaurav met each other in Gopal's room. They discussed the questions that had come in the examination.

" How was your exam today?" asked Haksh to Hemant.

" It was fine . My mind was very light when I started answering the questions" said Hemant.

"You had entered the exam hall after meeting Disha" said Haksh.

"Thank you for informing me about her location," said Hemant.

Till the end of the fourth semester examination, Hemant went to the hall ,where Disha did her revisions. He would wish her good luck and vice versa.The Fourth Semester examinations were over. Hemant and Disha had become good friends by the time the exams ended. Haksh was happy to see the smile on Hemant's face. He felt as if he had redeemed himself in the eyes of Hemant . Haksh was missing Smruti a lot. During exams when he saw Neha outside the college building. The girl would turn her face away from him. Haksh would pass comments on her loudly making her weep. He got some joy in hurting Neha with his comments.

Haksh missed Smruti, so he decided to return to Padampur after **solving a problem in Sambalpur . The boy wanted to shift to a boys' hostel**. He stayed in his dorm even after the fourth semester exam was over as he had accompany Gopal and the other boys of English Honours, who were going to host a farewell party to the seniors who were going to leave **the hostels as their final year of graduation was going to be over . They were semester six students, who had their final semester examinations in April.**

MAY , 2013
SAMBALPUR

After the month of April , the hostels began to be vacated by the students. Haksh filled up a form and contacted the superintendent of the Trust Fund Boys' Hostel in order to get a room in that hostel . He wanted to leave his dorm and stay in the hostel in his third year of his graduation .

Chapter 48
New task

* * *

MAY , 2013
PADAMPUR

After seeing off the senior students from the hostel and meeting the hostel superintendent of the Trust Fund Hostel, Haksh got time to pack up and return to his village in Padampur . Once in Padampur ,he was busy in bike riding and playing computer games.

After a gap of a month or so, the next academic session would start. The next session would mark Haksh's final year in graduation. He was not thinking about what was going to happen the next month. He had the **whole of May** at his disposal. He could spend the time the way he wanted.

One day he got a phone call from Chinmay. He responded to the phone call.

"Hello Chinmay , where are you now ?" asked Haksh.

"First tell me where are you ?" said Chinmay

"Why?"

" I have got some information for you."

" What information?"

" One day I saw Smruti in Bhubaneswar."

"What?" exclaimed Haksh.

"I saw Smruti in Bhubaneswar."

"When did you see her?"

"May be two or three days back,"

"Then why didn't you ring me and inform me about her at that time "

"I thought you would feel bad."

"Then why are you informing me about her, right now?"

" I could not keep myself away from it?"

"What is the use of telling me about her . I can't meet her" said Haksh feeling sad. "She might not have forgiven me for beating her brother."

"There lies the problem. **Who told you to beat Abhilash ?**"

" Even I don't know why I beat him ."

" How is your social service going on ?"

"What social service?"

" You were helping some love couples with the hope that someday Smruti would acknowledge your love or show some response to you."

" Oh about that," said Haksh scratching his head. "The social work is going on well."

"What happened to that boy named Hemant ?"

"His case took a very unexpected turn."

"Means? Did Disha love him?"

"No, not exactly love but something like love."

" Be clear"

" They have become friends. Madan and me were able to convince Hemant that even friendship is also a form of love ."

" **Friendship is also a form of love ?** You sound like a philosopher"

" Hemant told Disha whatever he had to say"

"Did they talk about the episode of Gaurav ?"

"Everything."

"What was Gaurav's reaction after knowing about it?"

"Gaurav loves Sandhya . He had no feelings for Disha. It was Disha who intentionally got involved with him. Gaurav had given some tips to Hemant because of which Hemant was able to be create an impression in Disha"

"Congratulations to you"

"Thank you but why are you congratulating me ?"

"Your effort got fruits. You were in search of a couple whom you could help. **Alok was an unfortunate case, but whatever happened with Hemant was something pleasing."**

"Yes, even I feel so."

" Let me come to the topic."

"So you have rung me for some other purpose?"

" Yes"

" I need help"

" For what?"

"For Elly"

Haksh and Chinmay had a long conversation. Haksh became thoughtful after the conversation. That whole night he sat in his chair and kept working on the computer for a very long time. He had a new task at hand.

Chapter 49
Railway platform

* * *

MAY, 2013
BHUBANESWAR

Chinmay was standing on the railway platform. **It was three o'clock in the afternoon. Three trains halted at the railway station.**

" How am I going to find him ?" said Chinmay to himself.

He took out his cell phone from his pant pocket and rang up Haksh.

The latter responded to the phone call and said " You just stand near the exit. I will come to you."

"Okay," said Chinmay.

"Tell me what are you wearing ? Casual shirt or t-shirt. "

" A t-shirt. It is a sports t-shirt from Nike company."

"The word 'Nike' must have been written somewhere on the T-shirt."

"On the chest. It is written on the chest."

"Then it will be easy to find you."

Haksh ended the conversation over the phone. He was among the crowd of people who had to go to the exit by walking on the railway over bridge. He reached platform number one which had the exit. He saw a Chinmay. The two friends embraced each other.

"I thought the summer vacation was going to be very boring , but you gave me a nice task," said Haksh.

"This task won't be very hard. You have solved a harder case like Hemant's"

"Every case is different."

The two boys left the railway platform and hired an auto rickshaw. Chinmay took Haksh into a lane where they left the auto rickshaw.

"Let me show you my dorm" said Chinmay.

The two boys walked some distance into a lane before halting in front of a three storey building.

"The whole building is a dorm?" asked Haksh.

"Yes," said Chinmay.

"Where does the owner live ?" asked Haksh

" A few metres away. He is the owner of **a number of dorms**."

"Great!"

" Bhubaneswar is a place where you have an excellent opportunity to do business. The owner has built the dorms for business."

The two friends entered the dorm. There were some boys in the dorm. The rooms were of various sizes. Some rooms were small , some rooms could accommodate just two people, and some could accommodate five. Chinmay's room had enough space for two people to live, but Chinmay did not want anyone else to stay with him , so he paid double the rent and got the approval of the owner to stay alone in the room. The room had a bed, a clothes rack, a table, some books and a laptop.

"Laptop ?" asked Haksh. "When did you purchase it ?"

"Last month," said Chinmay. "It cost me thirty thousand."

" How much do you pay the owner?"

" Two thousand four hundred rupees a month."

"That's a lot of money."

" Look at the life I live, "said Chinmay spreading his hands as if he were the Lord of the room. "Now, **have bath** and eat something. You must be tired ."

Haksh had bath in the common bathroom of the dorm. The dorm had some four or five bathrooms in it for the tenants . After having bath, he lay on Chinmay's bed wearing his shorts and a vest. Chinmay left the room. He came back after sometime with a polythene bag and some paper plates. He had got food for Haksh from a nearby hotel .

Chapter 50
Big planning

* * *

MAY, 2013
BHUBANESWAR

The boys began to eat the food . A movie was going on in the laptop. The two boys were watching it and discussing **their** problem . Chinmay did not have a big problem .In Padampur he always met Elly . Both were best friends. His problem was that he was unable to tell Elly about his love for her.

"This is very strange. You have been with each other for a long time. I have seen how restless you become when she is not found in the class or she does not contact you over the phone for months.

Even she becomes anxious when you are not in touch with her for a long time. In spite of all this you never told her that you loved her ?" said Haksh. "This sounds weird."

" I fear things might change if I tell her my feelings," said Chinmay.

"So what do you want me to do?" asked Haksh.

" Have you brought some amount with you or not?"

" Yes, I have got some amount . I got it from my brother."

"You are lucky to have a brother who is a contractor. Contractors get a lot of money."

"They don't get a lot of money. It would be proper if you say contractors keep the money. When the government sanctions money for a project, some people start eating away some part of the money.

The contractor is the last one in the line."

The next day Haksh went to the place where Elly was living. She was doing her B.Com studies in a private college. The girl was living in a dorm. Haksh told the guard about the girl he had to meet.

The guard called the girl. Elly saw Haksh.

" You are Chinmay's friend , am I right?" asked Elly.

" Yes," said Haksh.

" And you are Smruti's lover ?"

" Yes" said Haksh, "How is she?"

"She is fine."

Elly and Haksh had a conversation for some minutes .Haksh returned to Chinmay. Both the friends went to various places in Bhubaneswar for sightseeing.

" The cinema hall at Bhawani shopping mall and Nicco Park would be sufficient for the occasion . Confine yourself to these two places." said Haksh to Chinmay.

"But which one to go first," said Chinmay

The two boys were having their supper while **planning** something special. After eating the supper , they watched movies on the laptop. They remained awake till late that night.

Chapter 51
Shopping list

* * *

MAY, 2013
BHUBANESWAR

It was a Sunday. Haksh and Chinmay went to the dorm where Elly lived. Haksh rang up the girl. She came out from the dorm. She was in jeans and a top. The girl got into the auto rickshaw. The auto rickshaw reached the Bhawani shopping mall that had the provision for 3D cinema.

"You go and live your moment," said Haksh. Chinmay and Elly entered the IMAX 3D cinema hall that was a part of the complex.

Haksh roamed around in the mall. He looked at the various things that were being sold in the big mall. The movie was going to take two hours.

"What will I do all this time?' said Haksh to himself. He left the mall and hired an auto rickshaw to go to another mall. Once he entered the mall ,he took out a paper from his pant pocket. A list of things had been written in it. The boy **moved from shop to shop inside the mall** asking the prices of the various **things mentioned in the list**. After asking the price of the things mentioned in the shopping list, he went to the cafeteria region and ate some food. His phone rang.

"Hello, Chinmay" said Haksh answering Chinmay's call.

"Where are you?" asked Chinmay.

" I am in another mall busy noting down the prices of various things that have to be purchased."

"Good job."

" You inform me when you are coming. I am waiting for you."

" Yes, I will inform you."

The conversation ended as the interval of the film came to an end. Haksh had to spend one more hour. He spent the time playing a game in his mobile phone. An hour passed. He sent a text message to Chinmay. The message contained the name of the mall where he was in. After the movie was over , Chinmay and Elly came out of the Bhawani Mall.

" I have another surprise for you" said Chinmay.

"What's it?" asked Elly

"You like shopping. Let us go to another place for shopping" said Chinmay.

"Really! That's great" said an excited Elly. Elly's reaction is not surprising because everybody knows girls love to do a lot of shopping and are always on a look out for some source of money to spend it on shopping.

Both of them hired an auto rickshaw and reached the mall where Haksh was waiting for them.

Chinmay and Elly went to various shops in the mall. Elly kept purchasing this or that. When they finished the shopping after an hour, Chinmay had some bags to carry. The girl had bought some clothes and other things for her. Haksh was smiling when he saw Chinmay carrying the bags containing Elly's luggage.

"Now, let us go to Nicco Park," said Chinmay.

"But where will all this luggage go ?" asked Elly.

" I have a solution" said Chinmay. He looked at the door of the cafeteria . Haksh was standing near it.

"Haksh, come here" called Chinmay.

Haksh walked up to Chinmay.

"What happened ?" asked Haksh.

"Could you hold all this?" asked Chinmay giving the bags to Haksh.

"No problem," said Haksh taking the bags from Chinmay.

" Come with us to Nicco Park" said Chinmay to Haksh.

Haksh , Chinmay and Elly got into an auto rickshaw and reached Nicco Park ,a famous amusement park in Bhubaneswar .

Chapter 52
Pond water

* * *

MAY, 2013
BHUBANESWAR

At NICCO Park, Haksh was doing the job of a coolie for Chinmay and Elly . He was carrying Elly's luggage and following the couple wherever they went . Chinmay and Elly enjoyed the rides and Haksh kept looking at them . They entered the building that was a horror house. It which was made to scare visitors.

Haksh worked as a photographer whenever Chinmay and Elly wished to be photographed. The couple took various poses near any ride or other places in the park and Haksh would take their photographs . Chinmay and Elly had a boat ride in a pond in the park. Haksh sat on the bank of the pond with Elly's luggage.

"Helping a friend in his love affair is very heavy," said Haksh to himself.

"Thank you for everything, Chinmay," said Elly. "Today I feel very happy."

"That's what I wanted you to be. Every time I saw you here, I felt something was bothering you. You looked grumpy," said Chinmay.

"Back at Padampur, I was able to purchase things whenever I wanted , but here I had to adjust to the money that was being sent to me by my parents . I could not be as free as I used to be at home." **said Elly .**

"Let us enjoy the moment," said Chinmay.

He pointed his hand towards the pond and said, "Is that some fish or snake?"

Elly looked at the water. There were some ripples on the surface of the water near their boat. She kept looking at it for some time before deciding not to pay **any attention to it.**

"Whatever it be , it cannot be a crocodile. So, why to worry?" said Elly and turned her face to her left. When she turned her face to her left , her left cheek touched Chinmay's lips.

"What are you doing ?" asked Elly, taken aback.

"Today I wanted to tell you something which I have been trying to say for a long time," said Chinmay.

Elly did not say anything . She had a blank expression on her face.

"I love you a lot, Elly," said Chinmay. There was complete silence between the two after that. Elly looked in another direction and blushed. Chinmay was getting prepared **in his mind** for the outcome of his action.

" Focus on your career,"said Elly.

"You are my life, career, everything!" said Chinmay.

The girl kept blushing.

Their boat remained stagnant on water for a long time as none of the two was pedalling it. Haksh marked it.

" Maybe **Chinmay has proposed her**," said Haksh to himself.

After a long time, Chinmay and Elly pedalled the boat and brought it to the bank of the pond. They came out of the boat.

"Haksh , let's leave the park," said Chinmay.

Chinmay and Elly walked towards the exit of Nicco Park. Haksh followed them. The trio hired an autorickshaw, and it went to the dorm where Elly lived. The girl got down from the autorickshaw.

Haksh gave her the bags that contained all those things she had purchased . The autorickshaw left the place and headed towards the colony where Chinmay lived. All the way Haksh did not ask anything to Chinmay. He wanted Chinmay to narrate **whatever took place without any compulsion**.

Chapter 53
The mismanagement

* * *

MAY, 2013
BHUBANESWAR

Haksh and Chinmay were watching a movie on the laptop and having supper. Chinmay was narrating all that happened between him and Elly on the boat .

“So did she respond to what you **said** or not?” asked Haksh.

“She just kept blushing and said she would think about it.” said Chinmay.

“That means she has some feeling for you.”

“ Means ?”

“ If she **had** hated you then she would have become annoyed and shouted at you then and there.”

The two boys kept watching the movie on the laptop and eating their food. Haksh’s phone began to ring. He answered to the phone call. It was Madan’s call.

“ Madan, I am having supper. Ring me after some ten or twenty minutes.”**said Haksh**.

“That won’t be needed. The classes are going on, and you are missing important classes. Come to Sambalpur as soon as possible.”**said Madan**

“ I have helped another person in his love life. I am waiting for the result.”

" Focus on the exams. You have remained absent for a very long time."

" I will book the ticket for Sambalpur tomorrow."

"Don't commit that mistake. There will be a crowd at the ticket counter . Book a ticket now. The railway station always remains open. Now there will be no crowd as it is late night."

" Okay , I will see to it."

"Bye"

"Bye"

After finishing the conversation over the phone, Haksh resumed eating his supper.

"So, you have to leave tomorrow ?" asked Chinmay.

"Yes, I have to go. I have almost no money left with me" said Haksh. **"How much was spent today?"**

" I have not calculated. A lot of money was spent in the shopping mall" said Chinmay.

"Show the receipts of the shopping mall"

" Eat peacefully then you will see those receipts ."

" I had spent the money in arranging your meeting , so I must know how **the money was utilised**."

" You had noted them in the paper , isn't it? Isn't that enough to satisfy you ?"

"There will be a lot of difference in the price I had noted and the things Elly purchased because I had written the price of the things which appeared to be beautiful according to my point of view , and

Elly must have purchased things according to her point of view."

Chinmay heaved a sigh.

"You are hiding something," said Haksh. " Let us finish eating then we will see"

Haksh ate his food very speedily and left the food plate. He went to the bathroom to wash his hands . Haksh returned from the bathroom after washing his hands. He began to search the pockets of the jeans pant that Chinmay wore that day. He got the bills of the shopping mall.

" You have purchased a lot of clothes." said Haksh reading the bills.

" Not me . It's Elly who purchased them," said Chinmay.

" Eighteen thousand rupees!" said Haksh , shocked , on seeing the total money spent.

"Yes" said Chinmay.

Haksh looked at Chinmay with eyes wide open out of shock.

"Why are you looking at me like **that ?"** asked Chinmay.

" **I had got a big amount from my brother by** telling him that I was going to purchase a desktop , but after you have used a great chunk I don't know how am I going to save myself from his blows ?" said Haksh putting his hand on his head . He looked helpless.

" But you gave me that money to spend, didn't you ?"

" But I didn't know that you would spend so much."

Haksh could imagine himself being flayed by his angry brother over the mismanagement of money.

Chapter 54
Sleeper class

* * *

MAY , 2013
BHUBANESWAR

The day for Haksh to depart dawned. During the day time, Haksh did not make any attempt to purchase a ticket .He and Chinmay remained idle and slept. Chinmay was just thinking about the incidents that took place with him the previous evening. Haksh was sleeping to forget the problem that was waiting for him. Nabin had given him **money** to purchase a **desktop**, but Chinmay had consumed more than half of it.

" Chinmay ," said Haksh lying on the bed.

" Yes," said Chinmay, lying on the floor.

" I want to forget that I ever came here. I don't know what will happen to me if my brother comes to know about this mismanagement of money " said Haksh.

The two boys woke up late and had breakfast in a hotel. They went to the IMAX cinema hall to purchase two tickets for a movie. They returned to the dorm and slept. At two-thirty in the afternoon, they went to the cinema hall to watch the movie. When the two boys came out, the sun had set.

" At least we could pass the time. Now, it's time to

catch the train" said Haksh .

"Thank you for the memorable moments," said Chinmay.

The two boys returned to the dorm. Haksh collected his luggage. **The boys** reached the railway station. Haksh **missed the train as he could not** book the ticket because of the crowd.

Haksh left the railway station with the ticket for the train that would take him to Sambalpur the next day.

MAY, 2013
THE BHUBANESWAR RAILWAY STATION

The next day.....

It was seven in the evening , Haksh and Chinmay were waiting for the Tapaswini Express train.

"Never knew how the time passed," said Chinmay to Haksh.

Both the boys were standing on the railway platform.

"Time flies fast," said Haksh.

" The moments I spent with Elly were fantastic."said Chinmay

" You will keep thinking about them for a very long time."

The Tapaswini Express came and halted at the railway platform. People began to rush to get a seat in the train.

Haksh had made a ticket for the reservation class. He entered the sleeper class bogey that had the writing " D1" on it. After entering the train , he searched for his seat. The passengers in the sleeper class compartment were sleeping. The people who had got their seats in the upper berths , had opened their berths and were sleeping on them. Haksh had got a seat in the lower berth , but he found someone was lying on his seat. The person was covered by a blanket. He saw the person lying in his berth. **The person's feet** had anklets which meant the person sleeping in his berth was a lady. Haksh did not disturb the lady.

MAY, 2013
INSIDE TAPASWINI EXPRESS

The train had left the Bhubaneswar railway station. The windows in the sleeper compartment were open. The soothing wind was entering the compartment. The movement of the train was sometimes making the passengers jerk. The wind began to blow in gusts . A storm was approaching. The wind blew the part of the blanket that was covering the face of the lady sleeping in Haksh's berth. Haksh saw the face of the lady.

It was Smruti !

"May be my act of helping others in their love lives has worked," **thought Haksh** . He looked at the girl with his eyes wide open . His mind went blank out of joy.

Chapter 55
Joined hands

* * *

MAY , 2013
INSIDE THE TRAIN

Haksh kept standing in the compartment . Some thoughts were passing in his mind while he kept looking at Smruti. At first, he thought Smruti might have got some guardian to accompany her in the journey. He waited to see if anyone came searching for the girl. After several minutes of waiting , he found no one came to the berth searching for the girl which meant Smruti was travelling alone in the train.

"What an opportunity !" thought Haksh. The thought of kissing Smruti occurred to his mind . The boy began to imagine himself kissing the girl, but the next moment another scene came to his mind where he could see Smruti raising an alarm after being kissed and all the passengers in the compartment bashing him.

" Smruti has never shown any reaction to me in her life , so who knows what will happen if I kiss her," said Haksh to himself

His legs began to ache. He sat near Smruti's feet on the berth. There was gentle rain. Some rain water entered the train through the window. The rain drops were disturbing Smruti's sleep. She was changing her sides. Haksh stood up from the berth and tried to bring down the slide of the

window to shut it. When the slide came down it made a noise. The noise awakened Smruti. She looked at the train window and found it shut. The next thing that came to her notice was Haksh's face. All the sleep in her eyes was gone. She sat up .

"Is this your berth?" asked Smruti to Haksh. .

"Yes," said Haksh.

For the first time, Smruti spoke something to Haksh. Haksh was trying to control himself from shouting out of joy.

" I am sorry," said Smruti .

She collected her luggage and was about to leave the berth. She did not have much luggage. There was only a backpack with her.

"Listen," said Haksh.

The girl remained sitting in the berth and looking at Haksh with confusion.

" I mean no harm. You can stay in this berth. It's a request. Please be seated where you are. **I have been near you for a very long time. I do not want to disturb you**" said Haksh . He wanted Smruti to stay in the berth .

" It's your berth. You stay here" said Smruti.

The girl wanted to leave the berth, but Haksh insisted her to stay in the berth.

" I am known to you. It is almost dark in the compartment as all the lights are off. With which unknown person will you share the seat ?" said Haksh , trying to make a point.

Smruti thought for a moment and heaved a sigh . The girl kept sitting in Haksh's berth. She realised it was safe for her to be with someone known. Haksh and Smruti sat in the same berth. Smruti sat close to the window to keep the distance from Haksh. The boy could know the girl's intention. He just smiled .Haksh was feeling as if he was living in a dream.

"Smruti" said Haksh.

"Yes," said the girl without looking at him.

" Where are you studying ?"

"Government Ayurvedic College"

"Not bad."

There was silence between the two for some time . Smruti was dozing as she was feeling very sleepy, but she was trying to remain awake. Haksh noticed it.

" You appear to be feeling sleepy. Why don't you sleep ?"asked Haksh.

" My wish" Smruti shot back.

The girl did not say anything . She kept looking outside the window to avoid eye contact with him . Haksh could feel **she wanted to** avoid him, but she was with him out of compulsion.

" I know you are trying to keep awake as you are afraid least I should do some mischief." **said Haksh** and smiled. "All this is my fault. From the day I saw you for the first time , **I always felt something in me. I always** felt happy when I thought about you. I just wanted to convey you how much I love you , but you never responded to me. I always wanted to see you smiling." added Haksh.

The girl was not looking at him.

After some seconds of silence Haksh said , " After you left Padampur , I felt as if I lost someone . You just can't imagine how happy I am **to see you** after a long time . I never wanted to harm you. If you are feeling uncomfortable then I am leaving the berth"

He wanted to leave , but for some reason he was reluctant to lift his luggage. When you begin to feel sleepy , you are reluctant to do things . He left his luggage on the berth and walked away . He stood near the door of the compartment.

Time passed, but Haksh kept standing. Tears rolled down his cheeks. He wiped the tears and looked upwards towards the starry sky. The rain had stopped .

" After making various attempts to help love couples is this what I get ?" the boy complained . "The girl does not show any response. She remains like a statue. I thought just as Pygmalion got help from Aphrodite someone or some situation will help me in getting some response from the girl. She will never show any response towards my love . She will never acknowledge my love" added Haksh looking at the sky . He was complaining to God. Tears kept rolling from his eyes for some time.

The journey was long. It was nearing midnight. Haksh began to feel very sleepy. He could not keep his eyes open for a long time, so he decided to go to the chair car compartment and sleep. In a train that does night journey ,people crowd the sleeper bogey. This leaves the chair car compartment with not so much crowd.Before going to sleep, he wanted to say something to Smruti. He stood near his berth without looking at Smruti.

" If you feel uncomfortable with me and are unable to understand my love then you will never see me anymore. I am going to the chair car compartment to get some space to sleep. **A lot of passengers must have got down from the chair car .** There must be space **for me** to sleep" saying so Haksh, turned to his berth to collect his luggage, but what he saw next left him standstill.

He found Smruti sleeping in the berth. The girl had rested her head on his backpack and fallen asleep. Her eyes were shut. She had fallen into deep slumber. Haksh was left with his mouth wide open.

"If she had wished , she could have put my backpack on the floor and slept. But she chose to rest her head on my backpack," thought Haksh. "What does this mean ?"

A smile of ecstasy broke on his lips . The boy looked upwards, joining his hands and thanking God. His Galatea had given him some response.

About the Author

* * *

M.AISHVARYA ,who is fondly called MAVERICK AISHVARYA by his friends is a prolific writer. He completed his schooling at ST. JOSEPH'S CONVENTHIGHERSECONDARY SCHOOL, Sambalpur. He completed his graduation with first class and distinction in ENGLISH HONOURS in the year 2014 as a student of GANGADHAR MEHER UNIVERSITY, Sambalpur. He completed his M .A in ENGLISH with first class degree in the year 2016 as a student of SAMBALPUR UNIVERSITY, Jyoti Vihar , Burla, Sambalpur. He worked for sometime as a LECTURER in ENGLISH at VIKASH JUNIOR COLLEGE, Sason , Sambalpur , Odisha. At present, he is working in the DEPARTMENT of HUMANITIES at VEER SURENDRA SAI UNIVERSITY OF TECHNOLOGY (VSSUT), Burla , Sambalpur, Odisha, India.